One Night Two Souls
Went Walking

Also by Ellen Cooney

All the Way Home
Gun Ball Hill
Lambrusco
The Mountaintop School for Dogs and Other Second Chances
The Old Ballerina
A Private Hotel for Gentle Ladies
Small-Town Girl
Thanksgiving
The White Palazzo

One Night Two Souls Went Walking

Ellen Cooney

COFFEE HOUSE PRESS
Minneapolis
2020

Coffee House Press books are available to the trade through our primary distributor, Consortium Book Sales & Distribution, cbsd.com or (800) 283-3572. For personal orders, catalogs, or other information, write to info@coffeehousepress.org.

Coffee House Press is a nonprofit literary publishing house. Support from private foundations, corporate giving programs, government programs, and generous individuals helps make the publication of our books possible. We gratefully acknowledge their support in detail in the back of this book.

LIBRARY OF CONGRESS CATALOGING-IN-PUBLICATION DATA
Names: Cooney, Ellen, author.
Title: One night two souls went walking / Ellen Cooney.
Description: Minneapolis : Coffee House Press, 2020.
Identifiers: LCCN 2020002803 | ISBN 9781566895972 (trade paperback)
Classification: LCC PS3553.O5788 O54 2020 | DDC 813/.54—dc23
LC record available at https://lccn.loc.gov/2020002803

PRINTED IN THE UNITED STATES OF AMERICA
28 27 26 25 24 23 22 21   4 5 6 7 8 9 10 11

To Jo

One Night Two Souls
Went Walking

One

Once when I was small I asked my parents, What is a soul?

My father called it a mystery, like the genie in Aladdin's lamp. He knew I'd been reading stories of *Arabian Nights*. But what he said could not be true. A soul can't slip from a body and speak to you and grant wishes, if you rubbed yourself like rubbing a lamp. I had tried, many times.

My mother said that if she had to compare a soul to a character in a story, she'd pick Tinker Bell, the best thing about *Peter Pan*.

So I began to imagine a fairy inside me, curled up sleeping for most of the time, perhaps on a cushion of my guts, or some pillow of an organ.

"Wake up, Soul," I would say, but it didn't matter. I had to accept the fact that it could not be told what to do. I never had a clue when it would remind me it was there, whirring about like crazy, fluttering inside my rib cage, zipping around wherever it wanted to go, because of course it would do that; it had wings.

And it knew about the other thing. Like that was its job.

"The other thing" was what I called it when there was ordinary, everything ordinary, life going on as it does, and then suddenly there's a something else. I could never describe it to myself, but I could have called it "the thing that doesn't have words."

Once I heard a thrush sing in twilight, its notes ascending, its melody like no other, and then I had to feel sorry for flutes, whenever I heard one. Maybe the flutist was a genius of a musician, but my soul had learned a flute is not a bird.

In the waiting room of my dentist, a stranger suddenly smiled, and the light of that face was beautiful, when one second earlier, I thought I was looking at someone ugly and weird.

In stacks of the library where I wandered, where almost no one went, where everything was old and a little beat-up, a ray of sunlight came in, filled with swirling bits of dust, when nothing else was moving, and I saw it wasn't dust but particles of the spirits of those books, free and out playing around, like no one was watching.

Moments. They were moments. They belonged to the other thing and they could never be broken, as you can break a clock, but not time.

I would say to my soul, "Wide awake! Good job!"

But you can't believe in fairies forever.

The first time I saw the cathedral, on a drive with my parents, I felt I was looking at a castle. And then bells began pealing.

I could not understand why the car wasn't stopping so we could go inside. I *begged*.

Once I sat bedside with a painter who yearned as a child to be taken into the art museum he could see in the distance from a window of his family's apartment. Their building was in a neighborhood of tenements as far away from the museum, to him, as the other side of the moon. He'd grow up to have work of his own on its walls—but that's not what he wanted to talk about with his chaplain. He wanted to talk about longing for art when he didn't yet know what it was, outside of the sketches he secretly made, and how something inside him would leap and get excited when his eyes took in a flash of colors, perhaps in a woman's dress, or on the shelves of a storefront, cans and bottles and cardboard containers arranged just so. The funny thing was that the painter had no memory of the first time he entered that museum. His soul hadn't bothered to register the actual event.

He was nearing the end of his life. "I'm putting my soul in order, Reverend, like I never did with my studio," he told me.

I understood him, exactly, about the museum. But for me and the cathedral, it was different. I remembered.

I knew what a funeral was. My grandfather was being *laid to eternal rest*.

I had barely known him, even though he was the only one of my grandparents alive beyond my babyhood. He was an often-frowning figure who always seemed covered in shadows, at the far end of the table at big family gatherings, the first to be served, the first to stand up and leave. My parents and sister and brothers always seemed to put up a guard when he was present, which they didn't do with other people. Apparently he had a temper he was never interested in controlling.

"He's gone to light," I was told.

Entering the cathedral, I kept my excitement hidden. At last, at last, at last.

It was as splendid and breathtaking and lavish and solemnly gorgeous as I had hoped: four priests, eight altar servers, a pageant of a procession, the rising and falling of the organ, the incense mingled with all the flowers. In my family's pew, my parents were mad at my brothers for slouching and kicking each other. They didn't want to be here.

The altar was shining, all dressed up: embroidered white cloths, gold and silver, multitudes of candles, the biggest white lilies and tulips I'd ever seen.

I was going to find something out about souls! I was going to feel my own, waking up, moving about, in a new, non-baby way!

And once I did, I knew I would never be the same, like losing my baby teeth, and then came that first real one, poking up from my gum to fill the emptiness.

But after a little while in the service, I noticed something. Of everyone on the altar wearing vestments or cassocks, no one was a woman or a girl. I hadn't noticed that in the procession.

On the walls behind the altar were paintings, old, oils. My father didn't mind when I whispered to ask who they were. Before I was born, everyone in my family went regularly to church—to this one. Sometimes I could not believe how unfair it was to belong to a family of people who *quit church*.

The paintings were of Apostles, and they were saints named

Joseph, Francis, Patrick. They were rich with a vibrancy, an aliveness. They were actual men being shown at their best. The light around them seemed to come from the sun.

Then I saw that the one female presence was off to the side in an alcove: a white stone statue I knew was Mary, life-size, standing above a secondary altar, her gaze looking downward at vigil candles, flickering in frosted-glass cups. Trails of wispy smoke rose toward her. Her face was finely chiseled, and completely without expression. Her hands were at her sides, palms upward. Her head was covered with a stone veil, her body draped in stone folds of a gown, and also a cloak.

Even with the garments and the heat of the candles, she looked cold. She looked as if someone would be angry at her if she didn't stay still all the time, or tried to speak.

Meanwhile in our pew, my sister pretended to read from the mass book. Secretly inside was a laminated card that listed the rules of lacrosse. I was mortified by that, as I was mortified by my brothers' behavior.

But now everything was different. I understood that my soul had chosen this time to take a nap, after looking around and deciding there would not be *the other thing*, because of the feel of what was left out.

All the voices rising and falling on the altar were the voices of men. Clearly, something here was very wrong. It reminded me of when my brothers altered the radio in our mother's car, so all that came out was the bass. She would tell them she'd kill them if they kept messing with the treble. She would un-control her temper. She'd shout, "Stop turning off the treble! The treble has to be on!"

"I am going to be a priest," I said to myself.

I felt logical about it. I did not have a sense I was a little girl planning my future. I felt my future was already going on. I felt practical.

I had figured out that the reason there were only men and boys on the altar was that all the women and girls were at some other church. Or they were simply not available for a funeral on a weekday morning. I knew that my grandfather had wanted the bishop to officiate; they were friends. I knew the bishop was somewhere away, and had sent his regrets.

Women and girls were unavailable like the bishop. I felt that the altar was saving a place for me, for when I grew up.

"I will be available," I was telling the cathedral. It was as simple and real to me as my sister announcing, the day before, "I need a new sport, so I'm going to learn lacrosse."

Then at eight, I went to the birthday party of a girl in my neighborhood. A priest was there.

He was the girl's uncle. He was tall and handsome in a movie-star way, and he moved with elegant smoothness on the living room rug: the only grown-up willing to dance with the kids. Fifteen minutes of the party were set aside for music and dancing, which I hadn't known, or I wouldn't have gone. Michael Jackson songs were playing. The older kids made fun of Michael Jackson and mocked the songs for being bubblegum-stupid. But the priest showed everyone he could moonwalk.

A priest could moonwalk! I was awestruck. When he approached me, and told me it made him sad that I was playing the part of a wallflower, I thought I'd giggle like a baby from the joy that he was paying attention to me.

He knew my family. What would it take to bring my parents and my big teenage sister and brothers back to the fold of the church?

"Fold," I echoed, in my head. I knew he didn't mean it like what you do with clothes or a piece of paper. He meant it as the thing someone does with their arms, in an embrace.

I was happy to assure him that the day would come when they'd be back. I thought I'd leave it at that. But a burst of courage came into me.

"When I grow up," I confided, "I'm going to be a priest, like you."

I took his failure to respond to me immediately as a sign of encouragement. I thought he was silently urging me to tell him more, so I explained that after I became a priest, my family would show up in church because of me. I was different from them, I pointed out, but all of us were stuck with each other. They would want to keep track of how I was doing. My only worry was that, being the sort of people they are, they might not behave appropriately—for example, when I emerged on the altar in vestments, they'd clap and cheer.

"I'm trying to figure out what a soul is, to get myself ready," I said.

As I held my breath, waiting for any inside information the handsome priest might offer, I saw that he was looking at me with an expression of great disapproval, like maybe he was about to scold me. Inside my skin, I went prickly, head to toes, as if a rash had broken out, invisibly.

"Are you telling me you've had the calling?"

Now he looked a little amused.

I wondered, What calling? Was that my mistake, like the ringing of a telephone with a message meant for me, but I wasn't around for it? Or maybe the message hadn't yet come, and I should be patient and wait?

"You funny little girl," he then said. "Don't you know what everyone calls a priest?"

My mouth had locked shut. I couldn't understand what his question had to do with a soul and what I'd just told him.

He answered the question himself. "Everyone has to call a priest Father. See my niece over there? She's always talking about growing up to have lots of children. What if she said she wants to be the dad of her kids, not their mom? Wouldn't you think there's something very wrong with a mother who goes around saying she's a daddy?"

The music had stopped. When the priest walked away to join the grown-ups gathering at the table with the cake, I rushed to the door and ran home, and never went back to that house.

Soon, I was wondering about a new idea.

"Can a soul show up in X-rays?"

I was having an annual physical. I didn't know if my doctor had grandchildren, but if he did, I was jealous of them. He was a Sikh, kind and gentle, and the first man I knew who went to work in a turban.

On television shows that were medical, I told him, X-rays were always showing cloudy white shapes.

Talking about souls was already established with us. I had told him on a previous visit about my father's comparison to the genie in the lamp, which he shook his head at, because, as he put it, with great authority, I felt, there is no such thing as a genie. I agreed with him. I didn't tell him about the fairy.

He felt that my question was excellent, and so was my theory of an inner white cloud. But given the special properties of a soul, it was unlikely to allow itself to be photographed, not even with the finest equipment in the field of radiology. He didn't say what the special properties were, like they were a secret you had to be a professional to know.

"I'm sorry," he said. "But I can't order an X-ray for you, when nothing is suspicious about your health."

After that, I never mentioned souls again, not even when his stethoscope was at a spot on my chest where maybe mine was asleep. We started talking about hospitals and what it's like to go to work in the field of medicine.

The medical center I'd grow up to be part of was not yet built. My doctor's practice was connected to the brown-brick hospital where I was born, like everyone else in my family. Ivy was all over the walls. The entrance had an awning like a fine hotel or apartment building.

I never said no to going along when my parents or sister or brothers had to be treated for something—that was how I learned to say I'd stay out of sports. I could say I was saving myself from all those injuries.

My doctor felt I'd make a good physician. He said so all the time. But which kind? He'd list specialties, like a guessing game. For bones? For blood? For organs? For skin? I'd shake my head. He retired before I had a chance to tell him that the only one he never asked me about was the only one that was right.

Two

Welcome to the night shift, where nothing ever happens.

The medical center is huge in its awayness: steel and glass and stone, lights muted in the deep surround of the dark.

In the background are towers of firs that maybe remember, in their roots and tree-bones, how all this land not so long ago was a forest. On a moonless night like this one, you can smell some pine on a breeze and not know where it came from, unless you knew already—those trees are a solid wall, invisible.

Once at Christmas a high school came with a crane truck owned by someone's father. They strung lights in some of the boughs, and patients began asking for their windows to stay uncovered when dusk came hard and fast, way too early. It wasn't just the season. Night outside a hospital window, when you're the one in the bed, is not like other kinds of dark.

The lights were only there about a week. But before I enter the building I think the wires and bulbs are still in place, and juice will somehow return to the batteries, and look! There they are, bursting back on in little explosions, red, yellow, blue, white, green, some holding steady, some blinking like eyes.

I believe in expecting light. That's my job.

"I believe in expecting light," I say, as if it doesn't matter they can only be words to hang on to, out of habit, when there are no other words, when I am looking at darkness.

And so here I was, turning off my car, at a little before eleven, heading for the start of my shift. I was in my first month of nights. I was upside down and inside out, with the drag inside me of a profound sort of jet lag that felt it would never leave me.

I don't wear clerical black, but I wear a white collar, a full one, and lightweight clerical blouses in colors that more or less match fruits and vegetables: peach, celery, plum, cranberry, asparagus, yam, lemon.

My jackets are loose, in cottons and light wools. My pants, black or dark gray, have hidden elastic waists, like sweatpants for professionals. Sometimes I wear Crocs like the nurses, but it's usually sneaker-like flats.

Maybe, if you're sick or injured and alone in a room you very much want to get out of, the first thing you'd notice, when I walk in, is my hair. It's frizzy more than curly, needing most of the time a trim. The color is a gingery shade of light brown, no gray yet but I'm sure it's on the way.

Maybe you'll decide with my fizzy spray I am wearing a personal aura that happens to be part of my head. Or I might be wearing a wig, which was first blown about in a hurricane, then plugged for a shock in a socket.

My body has the shape of a pear. You may think I need to be advised to work out, but I get plenty of exercise walking halls.

Always, there is the collar, my fingers so adept at studding it in place, I barely know I'm doing it.

It's never off me anymore. It's there when it isn't. I used to think going to work was like an actor costuming up—that every room of every patient was a stage. In my early days I was frozen all the time with stage fright: all those faces with backgrounds of pillows, all those eyes turning my way, all those people in all those beds, and what was I supposed to say to them?

As if I'd forgotten my lines. As if lines had been written.

And back would come the question, thudding in my head like the sounds of a dull old bell. I like to think I know so much, and then I don't know anything. What to say when there are no words?

How do I do my job? What to say? What to say?

I believe in expecting light, even when it feels like a lie, because the eyes of souls see what plain old eyes do not.

Three

I arrived too late to make a visit to the chapel to sit in the hush and gather myself.

My apartment-for-one was in a development just a dozen miles away, but getting ready to go to work in the dark was still taking too long. Just before leaving I had a meal of toast and cheese, two plums, and plain yogurt with maple syrup mixed in generously. I had downed two large mugs of coffee.

Was that my breakfast? I still had no idea.

The drive is a straight line on our bypass of the nearby highway, but that took longer too. Stupidly, I'd tried to rev myself up—*because the rev is in need of some revving*—by blasting songs I hadn't listened to since high school. I had saved those CDs: metal and rap and anything like a tunnel of noise to enter and want never to leave.

I'm sentimental about the days when I was cool. I loved being a teenager. I loved pretending I was someone else and really pulling it off. I had put into hiding the me I knew I was, like I was running a secret protective service for myself. Like I was keeping my own vigil.

When I finally got my family together in a room to tell them I would train for chaplaincy and be ordained, my parents and my sister and brothers dropped their jaws, in the same way exactly, and went into temporary open-eye comas. That's how good of a secret I had kept.

Pearl Jam, I blasted in my car. Aerosmith, Guns N' Roses, Metallica.

I was driving to work like I was seventeen again, riding around packed in a back seat, toking on every joint passed to me, slugging whatever we had for liquor, barreling along old country roads with turns as curved as boomerangs while singing my head off, being invincible, like the night was the only place to know you're all the way alive, and who was I kidding? I was thirty-six and I was poking along below the speed limit nervously, like my body was impaired, like I was scared of the light of a bubblegum suddenly shining behind me, a cop on my tail. Like I had skipped middle age entirely and now I was *old*, all my systems slowed down, slowed down.

I didn't know the words anymore to those songs. And then I couldn't stop by the chapel for some stillness before facing whatever I was going to face.

"Welcome to the night shift, Reverend, where nothing ever happens and we're paid to sit around and play games on our phones, ha ha ha," a nurse said to me, my first night. In less than half an hour I was fully in on the joke.

All the same, I was hoping the hours ahead would pass like a smooth, languid river, bearing me gently along.

"May I not screw up anyone worse than they are already. May I do no harm that can't be undone, probably by someone else."

I never lost the habit of saying that when I'm about to go on duty. The new baby chaplain I used to be is inside me as just a small souvenir, but I don't think she'll ever stop piping up. If she materialized right now, like a little talking hologram, perhaps standing in the palm of my hand, in her brand new collar and a colorful stole and maybe vestments too, what would she tell me?

"I think your soul is broken," she might say.

"And you don't have a clue what to do about it," she might say.

That would make her a truth teller. I knew it.

But it wasn't as if I wished for a way to not be broken. Maybe I was too tired. Maybe I'd given up on something, in a practical, realistic manner. Out of necessity.

I wanted to call it quits. To accept I could not go on like this. That I'd come to the end of being here and doing what I do.

Every moment I didn't tell my department I was leaving was a moment to hope I could keep on going as I was, as I had become.

I looked up. A plane was passing fairly low, almost invisible in the night-clouds; the sky was too overcast for stars. I raised my arm and wiggled my fingers in a wave.

A man I'd sat with had worked in an airport his whole adult life, as a baggage handler. "Intellectually disabled" were the words assigned to him. He was a loader of incoming luggage to conveyor belts. He understood the reality of his illness—that it was terminal. Just like a place in an airport.

He hadn't asked for a chaplain. He explained he did not need a professional talking to him about what would happen to him when he left this world. But he felt that, since I seemed to enjoy his company, I might as well stick around and make myself useful.

He wanted me to speak to him as if he were about to depart on a plane, and I had accompanied him to a certain gate. I could only talk about what I observed there: a counter, seats for people waiting, the airline people in their uniforms, enormous windows looking out at the tarmac, a runway. I was forbidden to mention the checking of bags or having a carry-on. The thing about this gate was, no baggage was allowed.

"The gate of all departures," he called it.

It was a secret of his, but he had come to the conclusion a chaplain is the one you tell your secrets to. So it was good, he felt, I hadn't left him alone when he told me to please go away.

You had to say "all" for the gate of departures; it was there for everyone. It didn't matter who you were. People who didn't understand it would sooner or later happen to them were people who were *being retarded*.

He hoped I wouldn't get mad and yell at him for refusing to go along with everything you're supposed to go along with in terms of heaven and hell. He could never understand how anyone could think yelling and being mad and feeling bad and scared is *holy*. He actually knew of people, and not just little kids, who were so afraid of hell, they'd cry out in the night like they were dreaming of fires and the devil.

He did not believe in the devil or hell and that was because of John Lennon.

"I would never be mad or yell at you," I promised. "I'll be doing the opposite."

And he wanted to know, Did I know that song about heaven and hell by John Lennon, who used to be a Beatle? Someone who was nice to him used to sing it to him.

The song was "Imagine." In a weak, wavering voice, he serenaded me with a stanza—his own version of one.

> *Imagine your own heaven.*
> *It's easy if you try.*
> *No hell is below us.*
> *Above us there's always the sky.*

In all the years of his job, the same thing over and over, lifting and heaving the luggage of strangers, he had never flown on a plane. He was raised in foster care. From the age of eighteen, he had lived in a group home. Sometimes, in the van of a social services agency, he and his housemates went out for a movie and ice cream with folks from other groups. Or an amusement park or a lake with a sandy beach where they had their own section. For a while he had a girl-friend. He gave me a big, hearty grin when he told me he was not a virgin with his body. He was only a virgin about flying.

He didn't welcome questions. But eventually he accepted how curious I was about where he'd go when his plane lined up outside the gate, and his time for boarding drew near.

"When I leave my body and walk to the plane," he said, "I'll have a free ticket to fly anywhere I want, forever."

I made a promise to always remember him. He called it a vow. Near the end, he began to allow me to talk about myself, the same way someone waiting for a flight might turn to the stranger in the next seat to strike up a conversation, perhaps out of boredom—especially if the stranger was in a white collar. He felt that "chaplain for everyone" sounded nice, like a stretch of sandy beach that wasn't divided in sections, or a neighborhood where all the houses got invited when they had block parties in the summer and barbecued in the road and had contests, like the one with big guys picking up heavy dumbbells, which he had watched from a window, and knew he could have *nailed*.

He felt that "being ordained Episcopal" was nice too. He didn't know much about it, but they had to be okay, because obviously they let ladies *take the collar,* a good thing, or we never would have met.

One afternoon I looked in his doorway as I passed by, when his meds had increased and he was drowsing in and out of consciousness, and couldn't speak coherently. He was mumbling harsh sounds that didn't form words, in a voice that was somewhere between a groan and a growl. It seemed he was having a terrible dream, but in front of my eyes, there came over him a shine of peacefulness, and I knew it wasn't only from his drugs. I realized he was singing to himself and there it was, that other thing, a flicker, a glimmer, a piece of something that can't be broken, *real*.

My last words to him were about the weather: a blue sky, all clear, all systems go. After he died, I looked out his window at the white-out of a blizzard. The sounds of howling wind and snow made of ice needles had not come through the drapes to reach him.

At his funeral, a supervisor of his home told me he'd made a request of his housemates. Whenever they looked up at a plane, would they remember him? And instead of saying the dumb thing people say when someone dies, about wishing their soul would rest in peace, he wanted everyone to think of him and say, like a solemn prayer, "May his soul have kick-ass adventures, flying and flying and flying."

Four

Hurrying as I needed to, I had to pause by the linden tree not far from my entrance to pay my respects to Bobo Boy.

The season was early spring, the ground unfrozen enough for a trench around the base of the trunk. The linden is wide and massive, and a light wind was blowing, rattling the branches where nubs of new leaves were pale little polka dots. He had loved this tree; it was his favorite place to pee. It felt awful to me that the ceremony of his ashes-planting took place while I had to be sleeping.

Bobo Boy was a rock star at the medical center. I could almost hear in the wind the click of his nails, the whip of his tail in the air, the excited and urgent panting, for he was often excited, and everything to him was urgent.

That dog was absolutely unsuited to his job, if you looked up the normal qualifications for a position in the field of therapy animals.

After his training, he came to decide that no one should tell him how to go about doing what he did. He hated short leashes, but he tolerated a long one. He would not wear the usual Velcro-flap vest of his branch of medical services. He made it seem noble to put up resistance, as if an ancient canine code was telling him that a dog who wore clothing wasn't really a dog.

He had different humans with him at different times, taking the part of his handlers. The medical center had contracted with an outside agency that houses and trains the dogs who go out on assignments. All were sprung as rescues from shelters.

After an encounter with Bobo Boy, you could forget he had a handler at all. He had a talent for breaking loose, his ears perked up, and it would seem that patients were calling him to come to their beds, in a hospital version of sounds no human could detect.

A poster once hung in an outpatient waiting room. A receptionist with a good sense of humor tacked it up, and people enjoyed it, until someone official turned up to order it removed. There was a new decree that all waiting areas would only have framed, glass-fronted prints and only photos of scenes of the national parks, of which there are sixty-two, as all of us learned. The office in charge of wall hangings sent out a memo saying every park was represented, geysers and foliage and bubbling streams and mountain ridges and close-ups of flowers, and not a person or a creature of any kind. The memo did not say why.

The banished poster was made up of drawings by European medieval artists who created animals they might have read about, or heard of, but had never seen, not with their plain old eyes.

There was a crocodile, a lion, an elephant, and a giraffe. Each was put together so wrongly, so fantastically, you had to marvel at the accomplishment, especially when you realized the artists had blended in elements of creatures familiar to them. The head of a garden snail, greatly enlarged, was on the crocodile. The giraffe resembled a tall-neck donkey, the lion an enormous tawny cat, the elephant a gray pony with a trunk that looked a lot like a snake. You laughed at them, while acknowledging the strange beauty.

That was Bobo Boy: a drawing by someone a long time ago in a faraway place who'd never seen a dog.

He was small enough to barely make it as a lap dog: a chunky longhair with a body like a large form of pug, mostly a dark shade of tan, with lighter beige splotches here and there, randomly. His tail was long and wiry. His skinny legs seemed borrowed from a whippet; he was always looking like he'd trip on his own little feet. His round face, while making you think of a Yorkie, also made you wonder if somewhere in his ancestry, impossibly, there was a relative who resembled an owl.

He liked pillows. Many times I came upon him as he lay around the head of a patient, curled and looking proud of himself, like a hat with breath and a heartbeat. He had taught himself to do this after spending so much time with people whose bodies could not be crawled on or nestled against, due to surgical incisions still raw, or burns or other wounds far from healed.

If someone's head was off-limits to him, he'd go sidelong against the torso, burrowing in, so patients would stop worrying about their own condition, and worry instead, at least for a little while, they might cause him to be smothered. If they didn't want to pat him, because, "I'm not a dog person, especially when a dog looks so weird," they'd let their hands touch his fur, as if accidentally, to make sure that as he lay beside them, he was still alive.

I often went looking for him, to be sort of my assistant. Sometimes when he was sitting at a bedside with me, he'd be summoned to Pediatrics, or an oncology unit, or a recovery room where someone was taking too long to wake up post-surgery. If my bedside visit was a long one, for a patient who had no one else, and had entered the land of last moments, Bobo Boy returned to me with whatever he saw and smelled and heard and now knew about. His handler would go away for a much-needed break, and he'd place himself under my chair, wearily, heavily, sometimes sorrowfully. He would need to hide. He would need a break too. He would lie there as quiet and still as a pile of yarn.

He did not have the chance to grow old, although he'd been aging. The director of the agency came to see me in my office, to sit with me and cry. There had been an unexpected diagnosis. No war could be waged against the damage taking place in that body. The war was lost as soon as it began.

He was so good at playing dead, the people from the agency who were with him when he died tried to fool themselves into hoping he was pretending. But then as always, it was the moment afterward that mattered more, because the stillness kept on being still. They had waited through the winter for the trench to be dug, so his ashes could circle the linden as he had done himself, nose to the ground, so many times.

"Hi, Bo," I was saying, like ashes have ears.

I had heard there was another one coming up through the ranks. But I was in no hurry to meet him.

Five

Why didn't I walk away when I was banished to nights? I used to think people on the night shift were different from everyone else, as an owl is not a songbird. I know better now, but maybe it's a little bit true.

You can't pick what you get attached to. I never asked to be rooted in the medical center like a walking, breathing tree. It just happened. I was only supposed to be here a few years, the new baby newly ordained, eyes on a future in a small or medium hospital with maybe ivy on walls of brick, in a neighborhood of houses, schools, a library, cafés, a park.

Trees can be transplanted. There are lots of medical centers. There are smaller hospitals. I had enough savings to carry me through not working for a while. I had the luck of a family of people who would help me out financially, and never call it a loan.

Already I could have been looking for another "here" for myself.

The neighbors here are office parks, steel and glass and stone, ghost towns in the night. Everywhere the landscaping is the same, businesses and hospital alike: shade trees, paved walkways, carpets of lawns that are never weedy or sick, flower beds quilted with wood chips giving off their strange, oily perfume.

A budget ax had come out.

Our department was small to begin with, but now it was smaller than tiny. Those of us spared from the firings decided to take turns on all the shifts. But no plan for rotation was in place. I could say that nights fell to me because I'm the only one single and not a parent. I could say I'm the only woman. I could say a lot of things. When we were full we had lay chaplains and part-timers.

My place on the ladder was higher than the middle. Then the ax chopped all the rungs below me.

When I knew I would stay, I tried to blame it on falling in love with a room and my part in making it.

The chapel. It's not everything but it's a lot. I had taken up the cause of the renovations, so that the original box of a room expanded and turned into something that didn't look *corporate*, like a small, midlevel conference room that for some odd reason had chapel stuff inside.

I saw it turn into an airy, gentle sanctuary, sending out a message of, "Come on in, everyone's welcome, sit down and take a break from all the rest of this place."

I chose the new colors myself: pale mauve and a creamy almost yellow, the walls in two tones, replacing a cold, hard white that was merely several coats of a primer. Ordinary lighting fixtures became electric candles in sconces; the wood was upgraded to solid, friendly oak. The simplicity and the warmth, I'm proud of— the chapel became a home to me, not only for all the vigils that go on there, or the services when a service is called for, or regular meditations with Buddhists and all the rest of our gatherings, or the hours of sitting with someone in the shock of new grief, or the hope that a grief won't be coming.

I rest there. I have napped there and I take off my shoes if I lie down on a pew, my jacket bunched up as a pillow. It's the zero on a number line to me. It's the fixed, still point in an always spinning world where we see things and hear things and smell things and know things the outside world does not.

"We're sorry to give you bad news, but people here just aren't into chaplains anymore, not that we're saying we think you're completely obsolete," said the office in charge of the cuts, in more or less those words.

There was some type of study, carried out without telling us. Our resistance was futile. Our tries for outside funding were not successful.

That office is the same one I had hounded for chapel money. The faces are different now. The new ones are neither friendly nor hostile. They speak in voices neither soft nor loud, as if they took classes in how to talk all day in one tone only.

One of the lay chaplains who lost his job claimed he had counted how many offices there were for everyone who had nothing to do with healing and caring for patients. He said there were more for "the corporate business of the hospital" than for anything else. I don't know if he was exaggerating.

The head of my department in his usual way of being who he is advised me to remember we are ministers and *Please do not walk around mad like you're marching in a protest,* because it's our job to make the thing we call hope, and it's our job to make some light when light is absent, and look, here we still are, like the spruces and pines and hemlocks that didn't get chain-sawed, and we're listening to the wounded and sick, to families in waiting rooms, to volunteers who read and sing and put on puppet shows for children who will not outlive their childhoods, and also to a nurse, an aide, a doctor, an EMT, a firefighter, a cop, who has just seen something they can't speak of, because words will not come to their mouths, because they need instead to bow their heads with a chaplain and privately, safely weep, before standing back up and returning to duty.

It was now eleven o'clock. Showtime, as I used to once say.

Six

I am loved in my family in a sticky, primal way where one day they're all ganging up on me for being so different from them, and the next, they're gladly turning their eyes my way, because I entered a room where they are, and the pieces that did not fit together in a whole became suddenly whole, and all right again.

If I didn't resemble them physically, I would have thought I'd been adopted.

They will never stop calling me the baby. Or their pinkie, like I'm the tiny finger on a hand that does not have a thumb.

I was a late-born. My sister and brothers are so much older, it had seemed, when they all showed up for some school event, I was being raised by a team made up of a grandmother, a grandfather, an aunt, two uncles.

They have big personalities. They make noise. They are shockingly, robustly athletic. In the house where I grew up, stopwatches were in the silverware drawer, swimming goggles on a coat rack, trophies on shelves that in another house might hold books—and those trophies bore everyone's name but mine. I used to trip all the time on their skates, racquets, balls, helmets, sticks, cleats, bicycle gear, ski boots, golf bags, gym bags.

I never felt an urge to take up a sport or remain in a room where a game was on television. I liked the Olympics for the processions and flags. Until I was well into school, I liked being brought to the golf club my parents still belong to. I made friends with groundskeepers, and they let me run around in the mists of a morning, barefoot in the grass, slipping on poop of the geese who had not been run off the greens, laughing when I took a tumble, lying in the grass as the dew seeped into me, then jumping up when

I saw a crew cart on the way. I'd fist my hand and stick out my thumb like a baby hitchhiker.

My family loves birthdays and so did I until the birthday was mine and I was turning thirty.

I did not see it coming that thirty would be a wall I hit when I didn't know a wall was right in front of me. Where was everything I had thought I would have by now—a husband, a little house with a yard, a baby in a sling at my chest? And I'd bring my baby to work sometimes when maternity leave was over? What about all of that?

I had not been lucky with boyfriends, not in the sense of "this is going to last."

My sister showed up in my office one day, when I was running out of being in my twenties. No one else was around. She brought me an extra-large baggie of her homemade granola, to which she had added, special for me, chocolate chunks and salted pecans. Of course I was aware that something was up.

She wanted to take my photo, just to do it. No reason, except that she was looking through family pictures and didn't find any of me she liked, and please would I cooperate? Please would I smile?

She and I aren't sisters who go out and do things together. A week or two can pass by when we have no contact. We do not have talks with a beginning and end, a hello and good-bye. There has always been one conversation only, no matter the subject, left off and picked up, her and me, as if time doesn't matter between us.

She had never mentioned her interest in putting me online on a dating site, but I *know* her.

She said, "Brush your hair and take off your collar." She had read somewhere that men on dating sites would rather not respond to a woman in one, even men who themselves wear a collar.

There wasn't a photo. She wanted to take back the granola. But I'd already put it in a drawer, which I stood in front of so she couldn't open it.

I did not want a party for my thirtieth birthday. Everyone knew that. I wanted to go to work and go home with Chinese take-out and a bottle of wine and watch some sad old movies I'd seen before, so I didn't have to wonder what would happen or how they'd end, and I could just sit there and be sad.

Then there they were, on a Saturday at two in the afternoon. My department was having a special meeting that began with friendly cheers to me for the day. Then around our conference table we were all in serious moods. We were going over new disaster protocols: who would do what, who would go where, who would be able to double-shift if called for, and who wouldn't.

There they actually were, walking in, the whole original unit, having not brought my brother-in-law, my sisters-in-law, and at least a few of my nieces and nephews, which they had thought about doing, but felt it might all be a bit too much.

They brought a sheet cake, chocolate with buttercream frosting, my favorite. I could not believe how glad I was that the candles weren't those tricksters where you blow and they don't go out. I fell for it before because they always said that this time, they weren't using the joke ones.

The cake was made by a professional baker. The message written on the frosting was in letters made of dark chocolate, all capitals.

THE

REV

IS

30!!!

The zero in the "30" was a pink-frosting heart. My colleagues were up on their feet like they were welcoming a team of champions. How could I have kept it a secret I belonged to these people?

And soon it was a party in there. Of course they took over. They did that everywhere. It was jokes and sports talk and how my hair was always frizzy since I had hair on my head at all, and

I was such a surprise of a baby, honest to God, my mother was amazed to find out she was pregnant—she'd thought menopause was starting early. And this and that and oh my God, did I ever talk at work about the bombshell I dropped about converting to being a Protestant and going to *seminary*?

Shocking was the word for it. Always as far as it was known, on both sides of the family, everyone was a Catholic—not what you'd call regular practitioners, to be honest about it. However, that wasn't the reason for the shock. Had I let on I used to be wild? Was it clear to everyone at the medical center that I probably didn't even believe in any sort of actual, organized, regular religion, but that was okay because there needs to be chaplains for people who *march to the beat of a different drummer,* not that I'm basically a pagan with a white band around my neck?

"This can't be happening," I said to myself, after eating some cake.

So there was the "us" of the other chaplains and the "us" of my family and they meshed into each other to make one large "US" and they were looking at me like I was one of those fantastical beasts on the poster that should have been allowed to stay on that wall instead of a national park. Like if I were a dog I'd be Bobo Boy.

One thing about Bobo Boy was that he never doubted himself. He never wondered if the way he did things might not be the best way his type of things should be done. He was an artist at being a therapy dog.

I actually was saying to myself, "Maybe I'm an artist of a chaplain," as if that would make it okay to be outside the us-ness.

Afterward, I escaped to the chapel and sank down in a pew. I'd only recently started thinking about the renovations project. The chapel was its same old businessy self: an afterthought of a space, meeting the minimum of a requirement.

The sugar buzz from the cake did not last long. I leaned back in the pew, letting myself drift. Just a rest.

I made it hard to love me. They'd told me so. All of them, many times.

Why do you have to make it so hard to love you?

No one would ever explain what that meant. I was supposed to know already. Just by being who I am.

It can be lonely for me in my family.

I'd been at the medical center a year or so when my sister and brothers pulled me aside at a holiday gathering to tell me I needed to stop sharing so much information about my job. Our parents didn't want to mention it so they took it on themselves—could I ease up on the downer details? Did I have any idea how much I bummed everyone out? Could I put myself in their shoes and realize how they felt when they called me to ask how my day was and "someone passed" was part of the answer? Or there was a shooting or a fire or someone attacked someone with a knife, or someone very old and very sick and all alone pretended they didn't care they had no visitors?

My sister has a friend whose brother is a pathologist. Their family had to do the same thing with him they were doing with me, I was told. They'd be sitting around a table digging into their turkey and dressing and he'd talk about guts and someone's pancreas or something, and there would be *puking.*

Sometimes after a night shift when I'm in my bed trying to fall asleep in a hurry, my brain turns traitor on me and I'm stuck in a storm of images, like a movie on hyper-fast-forward: quick, flashing sights, memory sights, a patient I thought I'd forgotten, a bloody sheet, the face of a man in the moment he gets the news he's now a widower. Sometimes, almost asleep, I feel the hurt of "Don't tell us about your job unless it's nice stuff," and I half-awake dream I'm walking a hall filled with rooms in which certain memories of the last few years are stored, still raw to me, still fresh. I could call this hall "Rooms of Situations I Would Never Tell My Family About, Not That They'd Want to Know."

In one room was a woman who'd been trapped in her house in

a fire, and I was her chaplain. In moments of consciousness, all she said to me was how much she wished the firefighters had not saved her.

In another was a little boy whose father had forgotten to lock away his gun, and also to make sure it wasn't loaded. I was that child's chaplain. He was four years old. I had bowed low over him so he could pat my hair. My frizz for some reason had made him smile. For a while, it had seemed he'd pull through, but then he didn't.

In another was a girl of twelve. A few of her girl classmates poured a bucket of urine on her, after boys lined up secretly to pee in it, because wouldn't it be so funny, like something in *Carrie*? The girl went home and took a shower. Wearing only a towel, she ran out of her house, into the path of a moving car the driver had no time to stop. By the time I arrived at her bedside, it was too late. I was chaplain to her parents instead, listening to them ask me to pray that the people in the car that day would forgive their daughter for putting them through such an experience. After I did so, please, would I pray even harder that everyone who had teased her and mocked her and peed in the pail would go to hell and never ever get out, in case hell turned out to be a place you could eventually leave?

But I wasn't at home in bed. I could not allow such images to take up space in my head today, sleepy as I was.

I tried to think instead about how good it felt to imagine fixing up the chapel. An adjoining room was a vacated office space I'd make a case for taking over. It felt good to imagine a wall being sledgehammered down, particles of sheet rock dust swirling.

I sat there. Just a little rest, in the stillness. I didn't know I'd closed my eyes until I was blinking them open and looking at a pale, skinny guy I had not heard walk in. He was standing nearby, staring down at me, smiling at me. He looked as young as if he'd graduated from high school five minutes ago.

"Hi," he said. "Were you, like, praying? Because if you were, I'll just back off and you can get back to it."

A quiet gravity was in his voice, which perhaps had been part of him his whole life. The first thing I noticed was that sense you get meeting someone you know right away does not make fun of other people. I thought of an expression I'd often heard from nurses briefing me on a new, young patient, sometimes even a child. A compliment, always said with admiration: "an old soul."

I didn't mind that he thought I was praying.

"I was looking for a chaplain," he said. "You think you might have a couple minutes?"

This was Plummy. But he didn't have that nickname yet. He would give it to himself, for my utterance only, because the plum is my favorite fruit and his favorite thing to lick the juice of off my lips. He was a senior in college. He would soon be off to grad school.

He had come to the medical center to interview staffers in trauma and recovery room situations.

His theory was that people just coming to consciousness from trauma or surgery might blurt out something weird that happened to them while they were out of it. Maybe, he theorized, patients who were talking, lying-down zombies would tell things to, like, a nurse, in a raw, uncensored way, before they had the time to reflect on it and decide they'd keep it to themselves, because no one would believe them. Or they'd tell it later, so it would fit in with normal stuff people say when they think about *going to heaven*.

"Near-death experiences" was a phrase he did not like to use. He liked the other one: "out of body." But actually he called them *oobs*.

He had gathered no data. He'd been totally cold-shouldered. He had almost ignored the advice from a nurse, who he thought felt sorry for him, to go find a chaplain instead, since chaplains don't have the option of saying things like, "Do not even try to be bothering me."

The medical center is not, he found, user-friendly in terms of signs and directories saying where things are. Three people he stopped for directions to Pastoral Care didn't know where it was. But the fourth pointed him in the direction of the chapel.

I slid over in the pew and he sat down beside me, the space between us about the length of a standard ruler, which immediately felt to me like too many wasted inches.

He was into the science of the human brain, he told me. He already had the credits to finish college, which he had started early. But he was sticking around to finish some projects. He kind of didn't have that much of a social life. He kind of already had his name on a couple of papers published in, like, decent journals, and did I ever have a patient tell me about an oob?

Personally, he had never experienced any such thing. So he could be objective. It happened that the library in the town where he grew up subscribed to science journals no one else poked around in. That came to a stop by the time he was a teenager, but he had been looking for something in science that was mysterious and unexplained. He kept randomly discovering stuff about things unknown about the human brain.

Where he grew up, and inside his own home, there was an awful lot of discrimination against you if you were really smart, like you had a disability, or you needed to go through some kind of rehab so you would grow up to be like everyone else.

I think we both knew in a couple of minutes we were going to go to bed with each other. I think we knew it before I mentioned it was my birthday, and also before the inches between us grew a little bit shorter, and he surprised me by asking, "Why do you look so sad?"

I argued that I didn't look sad, as if he shouldn't believe his own eyes. I had nothing to tell him about personally hearing of an oob.

"Brains are so awesome!" he told me.

He loved researching oobs. They come from neurons and wiring! People have computers in their heads running programs that kick in at just the right time, programs they don't know are even there! But all the same it's unbelievably scientifically mysterious and so cool!

He thought it was awesome of me to be a reverend. He felt we shouldn't be bothered by the years between our ages. He was nineteen but almost twenty, and he was incredibly mature, he pointed out.

We were lovers for almost four months. He came to my apartment by taking a bus to the entrance of my development. We met nowhere else; we never went out together. He often showed up with his big backpack full of groceries because I never had anything he liked. In my cabinets he stashed Goldfish crackers, Hostess cherry pies, Pop-Tarts. He fried slices of bologna on my stove for white-bread sandwiches with mayonnaise.

I never watched him eat those sandwiches.

"Call me Plummy," he had suddenly said. Among his groceries were always plums.

Plums were so incredible, so supreme among fruits, he had realized: so tangy-sweet, so firm in the skin, so juicy. It was proof of the power of evolution, but didn't Plummy sound too like the name of a guy who didn't come from the middle of America, from a town so ordinary, its name should be, officially, Ordinary?

He thought Plummy sounded like he stepped into my life from one of those British television dramas where it's always a bygone century and there's a manor house, and though you end up rooting for the servants, somewhere on the show there's a dude who went to Cambridge or Oxford, and his IQ is off the charts and he's *moral,* and humble too, and everyone calls him something upper-class Englishy, like what they used to call their favorite teddy bear.

His mom used to watch those shows. Sunday nights. He'd sit nearby, teaching himself a new language to write code in, or blowing stuff up in a game where he couldn't turn the sound on if she was watching TV, not even if he put on headphones. He had not been allowed to have a computer in his bedroom until he was almost ready to leave for college, because his parents knew he'd never come out.

But naturally he had one in there. He scrounged up a pitiful Atari from a storage room at his school, from the days when there wasn't the internet yet. He sneaked it home and fooled around with it.

He imaged his first human brain at thirteen, when he created a Pac-Man rip-off. In his game, a brain was the main character. It had a mouth. It zipped around eating dangerous little villains who threw footballs like bombs, and just happened to wear uniforms in the colors of his town. The game was primitive and completely amateur, but there was never a chance for the villains to escape their fate of becoming, basically, cannibalized.

The only grown-up who saw it was a guy who worked at Radio Shack and let him hang out there. He needed to keep the game to himself, this guy warned him. It was a football-centered sort of town. His father coached at the high school. His mom helped out with concessions at the Friday night games he only went to because they made him show up and keep stats. His brothers and sisters used to tell him they'd grab him one day, put him in a car, and drive him to one of those places where families bring gay kids so they can be rewired from being gay. But it would be a place where they turn you into a football player, like it was run by retired professional athletes, and wasn't that a funny joke, rewiring kids, like it would work, like it wouldn't be some kind of torture, ha ha ha?

At fifteen he had a phase of being into nature. He built a game where you could form a tsunami in the ocean of your choice, depending on your skill level. It was tricky, but one thing leading to another, you could wipe out all kinds of places, even in parts of America that only have ponds and weensy lakes. You could target stadiums. You could tidal-wave a whole Super Bowl. He never showed that one to anyone.

To me, he could boast all he wanted about his old games. The first time we were taking off our clothes, yes, on the evening of the day I turned thirty, I did something I had never let anyone do. I let him undo my collar stud and slip the collar off me.

The touch of his hands was a whole new answer for me to the question, *What is tenderness?*

No one knew about us. Well, my neighbors did. But it's not the sort of apartment development where people make friends with each other. Many residents work at the medical center, but none were on my block. When I first moved in, I thought it was going to be temporary: the new baby chaplain in a one-bedroom unit at the smaller end of one-bedroom units. But every time I thought I should move, I just didn't.

"Your brain is as awesome as all the rest of you," he would say, and I'd laugh at him for how seriously he took me, all the time.

And he thought it was awesome I planned to never stop believing in souls, in spite of all the evidence there is no such thing. It's like believing in music if you're tone deaf, he felt. Or colors if you're blind to colors.

The coolest thing in the world ever would be dying and finding out you're not dead, he felt. Like one minute your heart stops and—wham—the next minute you're far away, high up in outer space, hanging out with, like, comets. And everything you wanted to know about, like, *everything*, wham again! You suddenly know answers to questions you didn't know to ask when you were alive!

What a dream come true that would be, he felt.

Then, when it was time for him to leave for faraway grad school, we said good-bye solemnly in my doorway.

He had postponed twice the date he was supposed to arrive for the start of the rest of his life. He had missed his orientation and he still had to go home for a couple of days to see his family. There'd be a crowd of them. It was going to make him lonely, so would I call him while he was there, and let him call me, even if I was at work?

"Yes," I said.

For about a month, I missed him in a general, dragging, I-don't-feel-well sort of way. I told myself I was maybe bugged by a low-grade virus I'd picked up in the hospital. I did not say yes all the times in grad school he let me know he wanted to see me. He called me a discriminator on the basis of age.

"Oh, grow up," I'd answer.

I did not love Plummy. I just didn't.

Not that I said so to him. Both of us were careful to not let the subject come up. I'd remind myself I never fell in love with him. Like I actually knew what I meant.

We promised we would stay in touch, and we did: emails, texts, phone calls, video calls. For six years. Also, I promised him that anytime I knew of an oob, he would be the only person in all of science I informed.

Seven

Of course we're not supposed to play favorites among the patients. I keep promising myself I won't, and I always do.

I knew the librarian would be looking at her clock, expecting me to come see her first thing, as usual. I would have to keep her waiting. I was paged almost as soon as I took off my coat and hung it on the hook in my office.

A patient I hadn't seen before was asking for a chaplain—and not just asking, but demanding one.

He'd been causing all sorts of trouble. Would I come right away?

On that unit, I met with a nurse whose husband ran an auto shop she was also involved in. She liked to compare everyone to people dealing with getting their cars fixed.

The patient, a lawyer in his fifties, was the type of customer who'd come into the bays in spite of the sign that said you couldn't. He would look at a wrench in the hand of a mechanic and tell the mechanic he was holding it wrong. He would order an expensive engine oil that was only expensive because of the brand name, then he'd watch it go in like he suspected they'd switch in a cheap one. He'd try to pay his bill with the only credit card they didn't accept, like there wasn't information about credit cards all over the place, including when you called to make your appointment.

In his brief time in the hospital, he antagonized everyone involved in his care, starting with a lab technician who told him that if she ever had to draw his blood again, she was going to take it all and he would not be able to stop her; he'd have to sue the medical center to get it back.

With me, as the nurse predicted, he was courteous and polite and even pleasant.

I found him calmly lying flat in his bed, covers to his chest. He was freshly shaved and showered, and wore a hospital johnny. The room was dim. He held out his hand to me for a firm, friendly handshake. I saw that he was not ill or wounded. He was scheduled for release in the morning.

I took my place in the bedside chair, and the first thing he told me was that he considered himself a rational man. He believed in facts, in evidence. He described his life as a comfortable one, well-ordered and satisfying, filled with challenges and a measure of happiness that basically, when he added everything up, came out greater than the sum of his disappointments.

He was quick to say he had little to complain about concerning his marriage, his children, his colleagues, his friends. In his personal life, while he valued the importance of emotions, he was pretty much the same as he was in his profession. He always kept faith with his powers of clear, careful thinking, and evidence, evidence, evidence.

He sometimes attended his wife's church, a historic one, noted for its organ and music. He had never cared for services. Church was where he discovered how it felt to be deeply moved by J. S. Bach and Mozart. He'd come to believe there was a part of the human brain that could be stirred only by a certain kind of music. Until three days ago, being spiritual was all about Bach and Mozart.

He would leave the hospital early, before breakfast. He had waited to ask for a chaplain until now, his last night, so he could wake to go home with a sense of something accomplished and done with, like a verdict in a trial that would not be appealed.

His overall health was excellent. He was proud of himself for keeping his body cared for, finely tuned.

Only in the last few hours, alone in his room, was he able to collect his thoughts. He felt it was fortunate to be somewhere no one knew him—having visitors would have been unbearable, for there was only one thing to talk about. He finally felt ready.

He delivered his story quietly, his voice steady. He was brought to the emergency room after feeling ill—he didn't need to share the details. All that mattered was the fact that he was taken into surgery.

It had all been uncomplicated, minor, routine. But while he was under anesthesia, something went terribly wrong, resulting in cardiac arrest. He would not bring a lawsuit against the hospital to compensate him for his ordeal.

At the moment his heart stopped beating, and before it registered on a monitor, he woke, floated upward, and found himself looking down at himself on the operating table.

He did not have the sense that he was viewing his body as a brand new corpse, lifeless as it was. Otherwise, he might have been moved to sorrow or anger. He looked at his body in an objective, impersonal way, and he saw that the man on the table no longer had a connection to him. Of the surgical team around that body, he took little notice. They had nothing to do with him, which was true of all the equipment, the cloths, the masks and gowns, the instruments, the sounds of beeps and chatter and someone telling a joke he didn't quite catch, but it seemed to be funny.

He didn't think he was freed from his physical self by any special occurrence, or the action of someone else. It all felt perfectly natural, probably the way a butterfly feels when it suddenly knows it will cling to a leaf no longer as a non-winged bug, or crawl on the ground afraid of being stepped on.

A deep, abiding serenity had entered him, along with the knowledge that he was weightless, like an astronaut outside of gravity. He remembered a thought that came to him as a revelation, and made his peacefulness expand to a level of emotion he could only describe as pure joy. It was not like anything he'd ever experienced before. No music was playing, but whatever was going on made him think that Bach and Mozart hadn't really known anything about music.

Then he went for a walk.

He had never been to the medical center before. Far from home, he'd been attending meetings connected to a professional matter. He was stricken ill when he was packing to check out of his hotel.

An ambulance had brought him. In the emergency room, he was sedated for his surgery. Nothing was in his memory of being wheeled to surgery.

In his new state, in his lightness, he was aware of the hospitalness all around him. He was eager to get away.

He went through corridors lined with doorways, many of them, the same ones over and over, as if he were trapped in a maze. The people he passed gave no indication they saw him, or felt his presence. He remembered a man with an arrangement of flowers in a blue vase that was shaped like a baby's bootie; a young woman in scrubs, pushing an empty wheelchair; a patient in a bathrobe on a stroll, while attached to his IV stand, the wheels of it squeaking a little.

He saw by this evidence he was invisible, without the mass of any object, which neither pleased nor worried him.

It was all simply natural. He was airy, he was light, he had no sense of time. He had no way of knowing how long he wandered and found no exit. But a creeping sense of claustrophobia was taking hold of him. He had never suffered from such a thing before. He began to be afraid he would panic.

How he was freed from the maze, he had no idea. He only knew that suddenly he was in the presence of a white cloud of beautifulness.

He was beholding a cloud, he told me. There was a cloud and it was in front of him, and in its center, somehow, was a light shining brilliantly, with a warm, soft radiance, unlike any other light he'd ever seen.

Looking down, he realized he was standing on what seemed to be some sort of wooden platform, or perhaps an ordinary floor, on which a carpet lay. The carpet fabric was light gray. It was splashed here and there with bits of white. He was puzzled about that, until he figured out that what he stood on wasn't flooring.

It wasn't as if he had feet anymore. He became aware that everything around him had not been made by human hands. Where he stood was a plateau, high up in a mountain range. The color gray was like a rocky ground, the bits of white like scattered snow. He had never climbed a mountain, but it seemed to him he must have done so many times. It was all extraordinarily vivid, right down to small details. He felt he had arrived at the roof of the world.

"I was standing on the roof of the world, Reverend. That's what I call it. But I knew it was not of this world."

Meanwhile, as he approached the cloud, he heard harsh, insistent, frantic voices. They were somewhere behind him, out of sight. *Come back! Don't you dare get away from us! Get this guy back!*

Very crude obscenities were also uttered, which the lawyer chose to leave out. But they made no difference. He ignored the voices. He only wanted to go forward. He wanted to enter the cloud. He now knew that the trauma of working his way through the maze was necessary. The roof of the world, of course, would not be easy to reach.

There came to him an excitement, a rush of desire, a whole new level of exultation. He didn't know how he knew this, but he knew that the cloud was a passage into infinity. What he might see when he entered it, what he might find out, he didn't consider. He was still too earthbound, but he knew it was going to be far beyond anything imaginable.

It amazed him now that when his heart stopped, his whole life wasn't flashing by him. He had never actually thought about it, but it had seemed to him something that would go on automatically, just because people tend to say so.

He had only one memory during his experience. He saw a glimpse of himself as a boy in a classroom, looking at a blackboard where the teacher chalked the symbol for pi. He was being told that the number for pi contains decimal places no one could count, because pi is a number that never, under any circumstances, comes to a stop.

When he was very young, he had hoped to become a mathematician. He was good at arithmetic. He liked the clarity and the evidence of numbers. But the idea of a number with the ability to last forever was too much for him to handle. He simply could not believe it.

Facing the cloud, so close to him, so *close*, he understood that he was finally going to know what pi means. He was going to become a pi.

And all along, the voices at his back grew louder, more insistent. He could not pretend that those voices were not a threat to him, and when he felt human hands grabbing hold of him, he was mystified and furious. He couldn't understand how anyone could seize an invisible man, and he resisted with all his might. He felt he was being cuffed and shackled for a crime he did not commit.

That was where the lawyer ended his story.

For the first time he looked at me directly. I wondered if he felt he had made some sort of confession. A look of relief was in his eyes, and though he kept himself carefully guarded, I saw what seemed a new lightness in him, as if he'd put down a burden and lay there with leftover traces of feeling his body had no weight.

We smiled at each other in the hush. He didn't ask me if I believed him. He didn't tell me he felt he was changed inside himself, as a butterfly can never again be a caterpillar.

He shook his head no when I suggested he might want to read testimonies of other such events and find out about research on the subject. His expression was inscrutable except for the softness of the smile.

Then he said, "I had thought, when I sent for you, I'd need help."

There was a pause. He seemed to think I knew what he meant. Did he want me to pray with him? Speak with him about a heaven that doesn't have to be called heaven? Speak to him about his soul? Or how he'd go back into his life a changed man, from his meeting with his beautiful cloud?

"I wrestled with myself about forgiveness," he said. "I was afraid I could never forgive my surgical team for bringing me back. But I have done so. I see that as a spiritual matter, and I assure you, I'm glad to be alive. It crossed my mind that the next time I'm in church, I should sit up and pay attention whenever they're talking about Lazarus."

"Because, from now on, that will have meaning for you?"

"Absolutely," he said. "I'm grateful you took the time to hear me out. I'm sure you appreciate knowing about my experience, exactly as it happened."

"I do, thank you."

"Please don't suppose I expect you to keep confidential what I told you. I only ask to have my name kept out, should you wish to ever share it."

We exchanged another smile, and bade each other good-night.

I felt that I'd listened to his story as the telling of a dream. I have heard many, many dreams. It's common for someone in a bed to talk to a chaplain as one would to a therapist.

The lawyer was not being monitored. His room was as empty of medical equipment as a hotel room; he was counting down the hours to his release. Obviously no one was worried about after-effects of a very recent experience that involved near death.

I spoke again with the nurse of the auto shop, this time about his condition. What he had was more of a procedure than a surgery, she told me. But if anything was bothering me after talking to him, I should see the attending.

I tracked down the resident assigned to him, a woman I'd run into before on days. She was only here filling in for a night shifter. She was frazzled and tired and her mood was not a good one.

"Oh, him," she said when I mentioned the lawyer.

She was hurrying to a room, but I learned that while he was under whatever anesthesia he was given, he had partly awakened.

Back under he went, followed by a little scare, a glitch in the proceedings, during which his heart rate was somewhat compromised. It was all just a moment: a slight irregularity, an adjustment. Just one small moment. The lawyer spent a few hours afterward in intensive care, so as not to take any chances. He was as strong as a healthy, middle-aged horse.

I didn't feel I was wasting time asking questions. I had Plummy in my thoughts. What to say to him?

I always knew what time it was where he was: Germany. The new baby PhD had been offered a position in a research institute he hardly dared hope to be recruited for. In grad school he had slacked off for a while—he fell in love with someone who then met someone else.

We didn't give each other those sorts of details. What he called slacking off, and what most people mean when they say it, are not the same things. When he said, "I am shattered," because of that girlfriend, I knew he meant it literally, as many people do not. All the same, his grad school experience worked out for him; he had rocketed through his degree.

When he phoned me with the Germany news, I pointed out that he didn't know the language.

"It's on my laptop for the plane ride," he said.

Sometimes, now, the six years since we were together seemed a long time ago, so that Plummy was part of the everything of my life in a past that was closed, and done with.

Sometimes it seemed only yesterday I was nudging him out of my apartment so he wouldn't miss his plane into his future.

The last time we texted, about a week before this night, he reminded me how much I'd admire the great hospitals of Germany, which he was in and out of due to the neurologists he was collaborating with.

As usual I reminded him of how I viewed him and me.

"Let me tell you again how much I look forward to being the minister at your wedding with a bride your own age," I had typed.

He sent me an emoji of a scowling face with a sticking-out tongue. It wasn't easy to remember that when I met him that day in the chapel and he thought I was praying, I felt he was someone a nurse would call an old soul.

Which he didn't even believe in. So why did I keep up the thing I had with him, whatever it was—back-and-forths, ex-lover to ex-lover, maybe sometimes not so ex? Why did it seem that whatever was between us could not be broken, like the other thing of my childhood?

I didn't know. And I didn't know why I decided, as I was leaving that unit, headed for the room of the librarian, that what the lawyer told me was not a story of an oob. That it didn't qualify. I thought it over and it came to me that his story was really a story of a man who didn't grow up to be what he dreamed as a boy he'd become. Like I was a psychotherapist, very intelligently and very correctly putting my finger on the root of a really good story.

It was all psychological. It was all about the brain of the lawyer.

And that was that. I had reached a solid, sensible explanation. The lawyer had figured out pi for himself. Plain and simple.

Anyway, I also decided, I needed to let go of the thing with Plummy. He needed to be more away from me than just living in another country. Of that I was completely, absolutely sure.

Eight

It was easy to imagine the librarian in her younger days glaring: glaring and frowning and staring you down if you talked too loud or committed some other library crime. She was a soft-spoken person whose words came out of her mouth with a backbone, an aliveness, an edge that was not always smooth.

I loved our talks, one-sided as they were. I knew that she'd always counted on making bonds with single ladies. Oh, but don't we have our secrets, men-wise? Oh, she was especially blessed in her life because her dream came true to have boyfriends and never a husband.

Lonely when you're with someone is different from lonely alone, she had told me.

It was five to midnight. She was two elevators and quite a few hallways away from the lawyer. I was a little breathless from walking fast.

I didn't first meet her as an inpatient. In my first week of the night shift, I sat with the parents of a young man brought in from the scene of a crash. Due to the location and the condition of his car, it was suspected he was trying to take his own life. There was a previous attempt, several years before, but he'd been holding down a job and seeing a therapist, and had seemed to be comfortable with himself, and hopeful and confident. The emergency surgery he underwent was not successful. I was with his parents when they were delivered that news.

Later, I walked with them to the taxi that would bring them home, although their own car was in the parking lot.

Back inside, by the ER entrance, I could not push my body forward in the normal motions of taking a step and then another, and I leaned against the wall, my head bowed. It was three in the morning. An ambulance had pulled in. The librarian was on a gurney, passing me. She commanded the two ambulance guys to stop. They did.

"Minister Girl," she said to me, a stranger. "I never saw anyone more weary. You go find an empty bed and lie down. I might need attention to my soul in here, and I want you rested. You go shut your eyes."

I followed the gurney, stayed with her.

She lived in assisted living and she had taken a fall some weeks earlier, which she had not sought treatment for, and didn't complain about, until a new night aide took a look at her and called 911. It wasn't that negligence had taken place, the librarian insisted. She liked where she lived—it was clean and bright; she had friends; books were always available. And no one was up anyone's back about who was brown or white or whatever, because by now they were all too damn old.

She could hide pain. She could hold on hard to her basic rule of never letting pessimism take over her soul like a force of corrosion, and then she'd end up in a state of pure rust.

An aide had taken her out for a walk in a wheelchair, on a day in still-winter that was unusually balmy. The librarian had petitioned for control. She could walk, although she needed a cane or a walker, and she was no good anymore at distances. She was still at the positive end of being frail. But she had arm strength. She took hold of the grab wheels, happy she'd thought to put on her gloves with leather palms.

All went well until she had to negotiate a curb cut. She had built up some speed while the aide behind her had a lapse in paying attention. A small front wheel struck the concrete curb, and the force of the impact threw her out of the chair to the pavement. The knee she landed on hardest was badly injured, but she was otherwise all right, or so she had thought. It seemed a problem for ice packs and ibuprofen and staying off her feet.

In the ER she was treated for swelling and bruising. She was X-rayed and given a prescription for a mild painkiller a few levels up from what she was taking. The general feeling was that she hadn't needed to come in.

Almost a week ago, she was admitted, and hooked to a drip of blood thinner. The clot that had formed in her leg was a large one, with every possibility of traveling to her lungs, to her heart. She was hospitalized for a dissolving, and why with all the tech and all the marvels of modern medicine was it taking so long and *trapping* her?

I had learned that at the age of twenty-two, she was the third Black person to have a position on her city's payroll that was not about cleaning, janitorial, trash collecting, kitchen work where you were never out in front serving meals, bus driving on certain routes only, and groundskeeping including the digging of graves. A Black first-grade teacher had been hired for a school of few white kids, a file clerk for a basement office of city hall.

She had not finished high school. She didn't go into the details of why she had to go to work at sixteen, in the warehouse of a mail-order company, where most of the clerks were Black. She did well there. The wife of her boss was a library trustee; she was often around, an anomaly of blondness and paleness. She made friends with the librarian, and said to her, "I think I can help you get out of here and integrate somewhere, if you're interested."

The librarian's first batch of years were in a back room, where it would have been excellent, in the minds of some other employees, and some other trustees too, if she'd stayed until her retirement. If she'd kept that place made for her. She unpacked new books, she sorted, she did repairs, she glued in envelope slots to hold due-date cards, and she ran a mimeograph machine for the monthly newsletter of new titles.

She plotted. She was acquiring skills. She ate, drank, and slept *the library*. She was proud of herself for never once going through with the desire to hurl a thick book in her hand at the head of someone looking at her a certain way, saying certain things—but leaving the back room needed not to mean jail. All the while she tended to her soul, as if she'd covered it with the same clear, tough, protective coating as the covers she placed on high-circulation books.

She moved herself out to shelve books one day when a cart of returns was overloaded and no one else was getting around to it. She just took a deep breath and did it. Later, she went on to the front desk, then scored a seat in Reference. At the time of her retirement she had an office. She had long ago put out the word that when you went to the library to apply for a job, a person interviewing you would be her, with some actual *clout*.

As a hospital patient she received cards and gifts and phone calls from her family, scattered and far off. She had visits from friends in her assisted living place, and a few women she had known in the library. But those were in the daytime. Nights were tough.

When I stepped into her room, she was sitting up, wide awake, her bed inclined. A book and her high-magnified reading glasses were on her tray table. As usual, the television in the room wasn't on. She wore a new nightgown, silk, bright yellow, ruffled, expensive—a wholly different garment from her usual plain cottons, which she called "old-fashioned nightshirts for ladies."

You would think from her expression I had done something criminal enough to consider calling the police. Or I had betrayed her by picking another patient for my first stop.

But I saw that under her glaring, she was feeling something else. A fragility was all over her, new to me.

And there was fear. She was scared, and I knew it, and it was coming from somewhere deep.

"Hi," I said. "I was paged for kind of an emergency. I love the new nightgown. Who bought it for you?"

Well. She let go of whatever she'd planned to greet me with. Her eyes opened wider; she was seizing the moment. She hated this nightgown! She only put it on because a niece of hers, the one who sent it, wanted a photo, which a nurse had taken on her phone, and the fuss was all too much! She wasn't one for frou-frous! What was the point of spending money on something real silk, when you can't wear it, in an assisted living place, anywhere outside your own room? The color was awful! It made her feel like a human daffodil! All her life she'd been allergic to that flower!

Yet I felt sure she loved wearing it. I sat down in the bedside chair, waiting for the ice between us to finish being broken. I looked at the deep dark brown of her skin, the cap of her closely trimmed old-woman hair, gray and silver, sparse here and there, dotted with tiny fuzzy clusters of black, like peppercorns. I looked at the hand taped and needled to her drip. I looked at her immobility. I knew how much she minded being stuck like this.

I waited a long minute once she made herself calm, and another, another, another. In the silence, it seemed the two of us were listening for the sounds of her clot breaking up, being vanquished.

Then she was ready to talk. And out it came about the broken submarine.

She will show me her soul as if holding it up in the hand unattached to her drug. I will see it's broken too.

And I will be sitting there, bowing my head, with nothing to say.

Nine

This was when the librarian worked in Reference.

One afternoon, the author of a book about sea vessels for spying and war came to the library to give a talk. He was a military historian. Ordinarily such events were not well attended, but the audience was large, with retired people who were mostly men, mostly ex-military, and mostly Black too. There were all sorts of college kids as well, having been ordered to come for some class, and a group of Black ladies who were top-level patrons and frequently lunched together.

Those ladies had seen his publicity photos. They could not believe he had not gone to Hollywood to be a star. That's how good-looking he was, and he was broad in the shoulders and tight in his middle, and as dignified in his bearing as if he wore the uniform of an admiral, not jeans and a tweed jacket.

The librarian was not supposed to leave the desk unattended, but she thought she might as well step into the lecture hall to find out if he could talk as well as he could walk and be handsome. Which he could. His voice was so potent, he didn't need the microphone.

She found the audience enraptured. He was nearing the end of his talk; then he invited questions. Someone asked him about a chapter in his book that described training manuals for living and working on a submarine. According to his bio, he earned money in graduate school by becoming a part-time civilian employee of the navy.

Not in the bio was a piece of information he shared with that audience.

Why he even brought it up, the librarian didn't know. The book was his first. He might not have been experienced at being such a center of attention, all of it quite radiant. He might not have stopped to consider the effect his words would have on people who were never in armed services. Or people who had never given much thought to the subject of submarines, as one didn't think of astronauts in way-outer space being possibly marooned, when the only vehicle capable of rescuing them was the one they were in. Or if, during the famous moon landing, say, all the fuel they needed to come home leaked out onto rocks and gray dust.

One of the author's navy projects was putting together information about how to escape a new type of submarine, reaching depths that had not been reached before. In a particular scenario he had to describe for the manual, the submarine had lost the ability to communicate its position. It had gone off the radar, and very quickly became no longer operable. All its systems were shutting down, when it was very much closer to the bottom of the ocean than the top.

"Now that," said the author, as the librarian stood alone at the rear, pressing herself against the wall, for she suddenly felt weak in the legs, "now that was something to give me some nightmares."

He described his paragraphs about emergency protocols, escape hatches, diving gear. One of the ladies, in the front row, put up her hand. She was not the type of person who speaks up, but she was obviously feeling the need to, perhaps for the first time ever.

"Oh, come on now," she said to the author. "Are you telling us the navy has air tanks big enough for someone to go from the bottom of the sea to the top? And like the pressure wouldn't do a thing to them, swimming their way up?"

The librarian felt suddenly chilled. She had no idea of the normal temperature inside a submarine, but she knew to be thinking, *cold*.

And she knew to be thinking, *dark*.

And *silent*.

The afraidness that began to take her over was something bigger and stronger than any bad feeling she'd ever felt. She was feeling it in her soul. What if everything everyone ever said about the everlasting life of a soul was the same as information in a training manual about escaping somewhere that cannot be escaped from?

"I think I know what he's talking about," said a man in the middle of the audience, to the patron who spoke up. This man was possibly a minister, perhaps a former military chaplain. He might have been wearing a collar that could only be seen from the front.

"I think he's talking about the necessity of giving hope," the maybe minister declared.

That emboldened a college boy. His voice sounded full of disappointment.

"I think he's talking about written-down delusions," he said, like the author wasn't even there anymore, and the librarian pulled herself away from the wall. She rushed away on wobbly legs and went outside for a cigarette, as she smoked then. She had three in a row, lighting off ends of two, which she had never done before.

Then she had to deal with a line of complainers in Reference because no one was in her seat. Somehow, she became absorbed again in working.

Many, many years went by. She thought about the author and his talk no more, until the evening she was sitting with a small crowd in the main parlor of her assisted living place, watching a movie. She usually didn't go to such events. She could not understand how her fellow residents enjoyed what the movie committee kept selecting, all that gore and fast action and guns and explosions, or otherwise the men would not show up. But in the parlor was a new wide-screen television. She was promised no violence and nothing disgusting.

It turned out that the movie was about a submarine, and she had to get out of there.

She did not sleep well that night. The next day was so sunny and warm, like the long winter was actually over, she went out for that walk with an aide. She had asserted her right to handle her own wheelchair, and suddenly, with the slope of a curb cut up ahead, she saw in her mind the tweed jacket of the author, the white of his teeth as he smiled. She heard him all over again saying "training manual," and she was back at the back of his talk, panicking, needing to flee.

So she began to speed up, surprising herself at her success. She had to get back to her room, get out of that chair, fast. She might have closed her eyes in the moment before she had to make a slight turn. She was not wearing the chair's seat belt. She was sitting on it. She remembered everything of her fall, which seemed to take place in slow motion, although of course it happened quickly. She had been afraid her kneecap was shattered, the bones in pieces that could never be put together. But it was still there, in one piece. She had rejoiced about that.

Then she became trapped in a hospital bed, having dreams she did not describe—dreams brand-new to her. She would ring for a nurse to bring her something to help her sleep, but she didn't like to take pills. Sometimes, the pills made her feel that a pillow of sleep was being placed on her face, like someone was smothering her, when she knew that no one was there.

Sometimes, she would wake with a picture at the backs of her eyes of herself in old age, as she was, frantically stooping to gather together the pieces of something scattered all over a floor, and the something, she would know, was her soul. Trying to pick up the pieces was like trying to scoop in her hands the dappled bits of sunlight all over the carpet in her room at the assisted living place, pouring in on bright mornings through her window blinds, which she never closed tightly when she went to bed.

I sat there. Why couldn't I be a good witch in a magical story, waving a magic wand, saying, "Look! There's your clot in the act of disappearing! And here are the bits of the light of your soul, jumping back together to be whole?"

The weight of my silence was terrible to me. I bowed my head as if praying. I was an actor alone on a stage in a spotlight, looking left and right to the wings for a cue, knowing that no one was there.

All the talking had really strained her. I saw that as she waited for me to say something, her eyes were becoming half-lidded, closing into sleep.

I went into the hall and found an aide to adjust her bed and turn off her light. I would have done so myself, but I was too afraid she'd wake up, turning her eyes to me once again, trusting me.

The aide told me everyone who worked in that unit admired her, and did I know that she felt she was lying in luxury, in her new nightgown, when she had never allowed herself a purely luxurious thing in all her life, and now she'd never go to bed again in anything but silk?

I said I was happy to hear that. Then I set off to see the surfer.

Ten

Stepping out of an elevator, I nearly collided with an intern I had nearly collided with a few nights before. He was a zoomer around the halls. Since he went many, many hours without sleep, he tended to make you worry, when he was stopped in his tracks and had a moment to be still, he'd fall asleep standing up, eyes still open, like a zombie in scrubs and a lab jacket.

Once again when we almost bumped, he swore quietly in Spanish, and I pretended I didn't have enough of the language from high school to know what he was saying. Then we looked at each other and laughed, again.

He wasn't rushing to a patient this time. He was on a break, and that was how I found out there'd been an elaborate and extremely well-catered social event that evening: a reception in honor of the medical center's latest new wing.

On the buffet table was a lot of leftover food the caterers hadn't taken. There were paper plates and napkins too. I thanked him.

"Buen provecho!" I said.

"Right back at you, Reverend!" he replied.

Next I had to turn a corner. As I approached it, I saw Bobo Boy.

He was coming around that corner at something between a trot and a run, a phantom Bobo Boy, nails tapping the floor, tail straight out like the rod of a propeller, head high, tongue lolling, ears waving a little. He didn't notice me, as if I were the one who wasn't real. I looked at his spots. I looked at the shine of his eyes and his little legs and his owl-like face, and I saw all over again how he looked so wrongly put together, and so absolutely right.

"Hey, Bo. Slow down."

No one was near enough to hear me talk to the air. I gave myself a shake, not quite the way he used to love coming back inside the medical center from doing his business in rain or snow. He would wait to shake himself dry until he ran into someone he'd have the chance to get wet, often one of the doctors who had dogs at home. They would laugh and laugh with him, as if raindrops or melted snow flying off the fur of a dog and hitting a target was the best thing to happen that day.

He never fooled me. I'd always sidestep him.

"Ha, you missed me!"

Then I realized I had to give myself a warning. No talking to ghosts. I'd never had to do that before.

Eleven

Ask me what's holy.

Two surgeons in scrubs were sitting at a café table in a side extension of the big public space called the atrium. The broad plates of windows behind them had been cleaned a little while ago. The smell of washing fluid still lingered. Nothing was on the other side of the glass but the night. The cleaning people could have coated the windows with black ink.

No one else was around. The area was for overflow of a lunch crowd. I was taking a shortcut through here.

The two men had not heard me approaching. They must have come straight from operating—those scrubs weren't clean. The older man looked up at me wearily, too tired, perhaps, to pretend that I had not just seen him caressing the side of the younger one's face, his fingers folded in, his fisted hand the opposite of the hand of someone throwing a punch. They were sitting very closely. I didn't know either of them except as familiar faces I had spotted now and then on the day shift, never before together.

A silver thermos was on the table between them, with its one cup. Probably, what looked like unmilked coffee was not merely coffee. The surgery they had come from might not have gone well. I noticed both men wearing wedding rings. It was clear to me they weren't married to each other.

"Hi, Reverend. How's your night so far?" said the younger one.

Their age difference was maybe about ten years. The younger surgeon was trim and smooth beside the shagginess of the elder, and he was completely at ease about being discovered. He was letting me know, with a smile, he took it for granted that a chaplain is not a carrier of gossip.

"My night," I answered, "is having its ups and downs."

The older surgeon looked up at me and I remembered that a couple of months ago I'd seen him in a restaurant, where I was having dinner with the man I had thought I would marry. The restaurant was some distance from the medical center, like all the places we went to. We had loved taking long drives to be somewhere alone.

Uh-oh, I had thought, spotting the surgeon.

He was hurrying by our table. He'd arrived late for a gathering across the restaurant, where several tables were pushed together for what was obviously a family event. Recognizing me, he briefly paused, saying hi, as medical-center people always do when we notice each other in the outside world. His eyebrows went up a little, I remembered. I think it surprised him I was having dinner with a good-looking man I was so plainly in love with.

The last thing I needed was to be asked about that man. I knew by now how to push out the thought of him, and in that moment, I was able to, so that it didn't leave a trace.

I shouldn't have worried that the surgeon would mention him.

"I heard they chopped up your department," he said. "That why you're on the graveyard?"

I have never appreciated anyone describing the night shift that way, and the younger man said quickly, "He's sorry for how that sounded. He knows how to say things nicely, but he turns into a little troll when he's way past his bedtime, poor baby. He can't help it."

That must have been a reference to a private joke between them. The older surgeon let out a hearty laugh, echoing in the emptiness, like the last drifting sounds of a bass at the end of a song. They went back to looking only at each other, forgetting all about me. I did a good job of hiding how much I would have liked to sit down with them, just for a minute, just to maybe hear an encore.

Ask me what's holy.

To my disappointment, the surfer was fast asleep. I usually found him waiting for me. The nurse who was checking on him told me he wanted to be wakened if he nodded off before my arrival. We both knew to let him be.

"Look at him," the nurse whispered. "He could be one of my grandkids. I'll tell you all over again, every time I come in here, my heart breaks."

The nurse was a supervisor, and someone I'd spoken to on every shift since my first night, mostly for brief consultations. She did not make a habit of talking about patients in terms of her own heart. She'd been an army nurse before she became a civilian one. She was a war vet.

"The colonel," other nurses called her, sometimes affectionately, sometimes not.

On my shift the night before, she confided in me, personally, confidentially, in the hall outside this room. So our face-to-face by the surfer's bed needed an acknowledgment. There had to be a moment of figuring out if the ground between us had shifted and we needed to deal with it.

There was something helmet-like in the short gray flatness of her haircut, something corduroy-like in the face so lined with wrinkles. I needed a signal from her about whether or not she wanted me to encourage her to speak privately, more than she already had.

She was done with it, she was telling me, with a look. She was back to being professional, nurse to chaplain, let's carry on the same as always. I was the only person in the medical center who now knew that a year ago, suddenly, she became a widow. She and her husband had been married for thirty-two years.

His death was the reason she had applied to work nights. Her job before this was in a daytime clinic. She wasn't ready to retire, and in the early shock of her grief, she felt hopeless about how she'd get through the next few years.

But she learned that by sleeping at home in the daytime, she could imagine that her husband, who had retired already, was puttering around in their garage; he was a woodworking hobby-ist. Or he'd gone off to buy a new pair of shoes, or he was swimming at the Y, which was something he had planned to take up.

She told me she had never known before what powers she had for creating a delusion, and then calling it reality—she had thought that anyone who was ever in a war couldn't possibly have delusions about anything at all.

And she had asked me if I personally had any idea what it's like to love a man you believe you'll be spending your whole life with, and the day arrives that becomes the worst day you'll ever endure, because all of a sudden, he's not there.

As soon as she asked the question, she apologized for it. We knew she had not been speaking to me as someone she hoped to be personal friends with. She was someone talking to her minister, which she had temporarily assigned me to be.

Now I was whispering to her, "I wish I could have made it to see him sooner. Did that aide who promised to bring him tacos come through?"

The colonel peered down at the boy in the bed with the steely gaze she was well known for. It softened one second later.

"Don't get me going, Reverend, on what all of them are bringing him. He goes off a liquid diet and they're writing down requests, but yes, he had tacos for dinner. And a strawberry shake. And cookies. If you want to sit awhile, and he throws up, don't feel sorry for him. Crank up the bed so he doesn't gag, and hit the buzzer."

"I will," I said.

Alone with him, I couldn't help wishing he'd stir. He slept in the daytime on and off, being interested in staying awake at night as long as he could. I knew that had already started changing. Sleeping through the days had meant not being aware he had no visitors.

He was fifteen. Pale downy hair was sprouting on the head shaved bald for what he'd lately been calling a few little minor repairs, no big deal. He seemed to want to think of his brain as an everyday gadget that had needed a little fixing.

There had been a great fear he would never again be able to talk. Or, if able to, he would have the abilities of a baby, or a toddler who might never understand what the alphabet is, or learn how to count on his own fingers.

Under the bedclothes his body looked whole, undamaged. Asleep, he could have been a teenager who thought it would be fun to be bald. He could have been anyone who would wake in the morning and swing legs to the side of a bed and place two feet on the floor, then stand and go have another day.

Before he was moved from the brain trauma unit to his private room, he woke and amazed everyone. "Hi! What's happening? Where am I?"

There had been forms to fill out. He dictated the answers. Whoever typed his replies might have been the parent of a teen, for they ended up in his file with a verbatim dramatic flair. Did he have a religious affiliation? A church he went to? WHO, ME? HA HA HA! NO WAY! Would he like a visit from a hospital chaplain? GET OUT LIKE ARE YOU KIDDING ME WITH THAT?

But he was alone.

He had his own credit card. Without telling anyone, he flew east from his home in Southern California to visit a friend in a boarding school. He was not reported missing, as there was no one to make such a report. His own school thought he'd been away for the funeral of a family member. The maid and the cook in his household knew he'd be staying with a friend, but they thought he meant someone right down the road.

It was a Saturday night when the catastrophe took place. Years ago, that school had a custom of sophomores going out on their own to an old, abandoned granite quarry, for some hiking and climbing by the light of a full moon. It was a rite of passage sort of thing. At the top of a cliffside, proud of yourself for daring to meet a challenge, you waited to watch the sun rise, and then returned to the school as part of a legend.

Someone had the idea to revive the custom. The boys who set

out for the adventure that night were different from those of the past: they weren't popular with anyone except each other, and they did not belong to rugby or soccer teams, or any teams whatsoever. And they had phones to take photos and videos.

The surfer went along; he didn't know what else to do with himself. In California, his friend had taken a class at an indoor rock-climbing school, so it wasn't as if he was being reckless. He'd just follow the lead of his friend.

A ledge they were all standing on had collapsed. There were six boys. He was the only one to survive the fall.

His phone, in his pocket, was shattered. He had no ID with him. He'd been staying in the dorm of his friend sort of secretly—it took a while to find out who he was. And then his parents were hard to reach.

They had separated. The one who was in charge of him had gone through some sort of crisis, and had entered a private treatment center where they didn't let patients have contact with outsiders. The other parent, who seemed not to know about that, was somewhere remote, working on a documentary with a movie production company. A message came to the medical center that the faraway parent was being plagued by bad weather, and was emotionally demolished about the news and sorry to not be around, but overjoyed that he'd made it out alive.

He was an only child. An aunt and uncle in California called to say they were working on making the trip to visit him, as temporary proxy parents. They would arrange to fly him back via private plane as soon as possible. But they kept not showing up.

He was out of Brain Trauma and fully alert when I first sat with him. He knew that what lay ahead for him was a residential care facility, where he'd enter into all sorts of therapies. He knew what had happened to his friend and those other boys. He did not let on he understood the extent of his injuries.

A social worker and someone from Psychiatry were assigned to him. He refused to talk about that Saturday night. Or about his parents. Withdrawing into himself, he seemed to decide the best thing to do was to imagine there'd been no such place as the quarry, and he never went up on rocks to see his first-ever East Coast sunrise.

No one at the medical center knew he was a surfer. I ended up with the credit for breaking through to him, but it didn't have anything to do with me, beyond the facts that I kept showing up in his room, and once, I mentioned to him how he reminded me of someone I knew, someone I was personally fond of, older than he was, but not by an awful lot.

The surfer gave me a goofy, lopsided smile when I told him the nickname of that person was kind of the name of a fruit. Maybe someday, I had suggested, I'd talk to him a little more about that person—but I never did. It seemed enough to him that I had used the word "fond" in a connection to himself.

The breakthrough happened because the colonel bribed him. I was not supposed to know about this, but he couldn't stand not telling me. She had sworn to him that if he let me be his chaplain, she would make him the peanut butter pie she made at home for her grandchildren.

He had never heard of peanut butter pie before. Peanut butter pie was awesome. He was almost addicted to it. The top, he described, was solid chocolate. The crust was made of graham crackers the colonel put in a bag and *hammered*. Every couple of bites, totally randomly, he came upon, guess what, *embedded baked-in mini Reese's Cups*. It was a genius of a thing to get to eat! I was not allowed to tell the colonel I knew about the pie. He was trusting me with a confidence. He didn't tell me it was a test for me, but it was.

One night he asked me if it was hard to be forced to be celibate. I didn't laugh. He meant it seriously. I explained that the church I was ordained in lets clergy do pretty much anything they want to, within reason.

Did I have a husband, or a boyfriend?

I had shaken my head. The truth.

If I had a boyfriend, would I bring him in, if he'd go out in the middle of night, so he, the surfer, could meet him, and see if he was decent or something, just to check?

Yes. I would do that.

When I was his age, did I know anyone that I, like, grew up with, and they were my only friend and they died?

I had not had that experience. Did he want to talk about it?

No, he was only being abstract, like the question just popped into his head. And by the way, it was interesting that, if I wasn't kind of old, but not, like, *old,* just more like, grown up, I'd look just like Annie in *Annie,* for having kind of the same hair. He had noticed that. Did I know what he meant, that dumb movie, but the orphan girl was kind of all right?

I knew what he meant, yes, thanks a lot for putting that song in my head.

Right, that song. Tomorrow and the sun coming up and bet your bottom dollar. That song sucked. Was it okay to say "sucked"?

Sure. He could say anything he wanted.

It was something like a little after midnight when we had that conversation. The colonel strode in, looked around, and strode out, probably needing to see for herself if he was keeping his part of the pie bargain.

By then he was looking tired. He had started receiving visitors in the daytime: student nurses on their breaks, a guy in Maintenance who grew up in Los Angeles, teenage girls who came to the medical center after school as volunteers. I knew it wasn't all about feeling sorry for him, for being so pale and broken and needy. It wasn't about how he was connected to a tragedy that for a couple of days was all over the news.

I had heard that a TV show displayed photos posted online by a couple of the boarding-school boys, when their ascent up the rocks was beginning. They were laughing. The light flashes from their phones made it seem they were shining, as if brightly lit up by white flares.

There was something about him I hadn't been able to describe to myself. I wasn't sure what it was. But something under his surface was very, very strong. It was almost magnetic, in a way. I felt that his soul was powerful and unbreakable, as a wave breaks, yet still remains water.

He was really the one who took care of making a connection with me. I had said it was okay to say the word "sucked," and there he lay, fighting with himself to keep his eyes open. He reminded me of little kids in Pediatrics insisting they do not need a nap, because someone's coming for a story hour, or there's going to be a puppet show or someone singing, and they don't want to miss out on the pleasure of the waiting.

But then he looked more awake than he ever had before. For a moment full of dread to me, I wondered if he might ask me, Did I believe he'd ever be able to walk again?

"Ask me what's holy," he said.

I expected a teenager-cynical remark from a boy with a need to say something offensive. I would not have held it against him.

"Okay," I said. "What's holy?"

"Waves," he answered.

"Okay again. What kind of waves?"

"The kind that come to life in the Pacific Ocean."

His parents bought him his first board, a beginner one for babies, when he was nine. They weren't surfers or even swimmers. The ocean was what you looked at from your deck and your windows. They had predicted he wouldn't stick with this new thing, as he hadn't stuck with anything he had asked them to buy him, like the camera that cost a fortune when he wanted to learn photography, and the four-wheeler he had wanted to ride in the hills. He never took the camera from its box. The four-wheeler, he stalled the first time he was on it; he never went near it again.

He didn't know how he knew he belonged on a surfboard. You know how there are newborn turtles that crack out of their eggs in the sand and go right on a rush to the water, when they don't even know what an ocean is, being like two minutes old? It was like that.

"I'm learning how to surf in my head now. I wanted you to know that," he said.

When I left his room that night, I went to my office and turned on my computer, a desktop, wide-screened. I looked up surfing things. I learned these words: hollow, tube, clean, glassy, messy, point break, A-frame, peak. I went on YouTube and watched the trailer for *The Endless Summer*. When I reported that, he told me it was the greatest surfer movie ever made, even though it was so old, it was ancient.

But on this night he didn't even flicker his eyelids as I watched him sleep. Sooner or later he would be wheeled on a gurney, out of the medical center. I knew it was going to hurt to say good-bye to him.

I turned to leave his room. The theme music of *The Endless Summer* had just come into my head, so I was walking the hallway to the sounds of those strings, rolling along, the guitars like voices, talking about air and sunlight and paddling out on a board, and how cool it was to be part of an ocean, watching and waiting for a perfect wave.

Right away, as if a radio played, and the next song came abruptly, way too early, I heard the swell of the background-music orchestra in *The Hunt for Red October*.

It occurred to me this might have been the film the librarian didn't watch, because it's all about a submarine.

I know that movie very well. Plummy brought it to my apartment on DVD. I only just then thought of it. He made me watch it with him something like three times. I had to poke him in the ribs to get him to stop saying lines along with the actors, even when the words were in Russian. It's the best movie about a submarine ever made, he had told me, even though it's so old.

"This is a strange night," I was saying to myself.

I went all the way back to the room of the librarian. Her sleep-breathing was regular, easygoing. In the soft slack of her face she looked untroubled. I breathed a wish that her dreams were good ones.

I wrote a note on the whiteboard that's supposed to be only for medical notes.

"See you before I go off duty," I wrote, as if I had any idea what I'd say to her about the broken pieces of her soul.

"Love, your chaplain," I wrote.

Twelve

The gift shop in the night was as frozen and dim as any store in its downtime. I was passing by on my way to the new wing for free food—passing in a hurry, as I'd done countless times before. I happened to turn my head in the direction of the window displays. This was a random, accidental thing.

It was sitting on a shelf: a blue vase in the shape of a baby's bootie.

The shelf was crowded. The vase was wedged between an oversize coffee mug covered with smiley faces and another vase: a bug-eyed, green-and-yellow frog, which for some reason wore a red bow tie. Compared to those objects, the bootie was small and almost boring. No flowers were in its hollow, but then, the flowers they sell are kept in a separate area.

To fit the vase, stems of most flowers would need to be trimmed short. The flowers would be small, perhaps with buds the sizes of buttons. The shade of blue was light, pastel. Probably the vase was porcelain. Something about the texture made it look as if it were knitted.

I had come to a stop. Within the shop were balloons on ribbons of strings, popular with visitors who tie them to beds of patients. Get well soon! More smiley faces. Pink ones. Blue ones. Congratulations! Yellow ones, meant to signify sunshine. Red ones in the shape of a Valentine heart. A cartoon one of a dog with a caption of "BE GOOD AND HEEL," and a line through the second "E." An "A" was just above it.

A few balloons were white and tinsel-silver. They looked shiny in the shadows: round little clouds of an indoor sky.

I re-heard the lawyer's voice, steady, confident: a presentation of evidence.

I saw a man carrying flowers in a blue vase that was shaped like a baby's bootie.

Yet the lawyer had not been anywhere near here, unless he'd left his bed in his unit, in his hospital johnny, for a walk through the halls, all the way to the gift shop. And he had seen the bootie vase, and then it turned up in the story he told me, a story like a story of a dream.

There wasn't really that "unless." He could not have taken a walk that had placed him where I was standing. He could not have looked at the shelf I was looking at.

I decided he must have seen, perhaps when he was being brought into the hospital, someone who had purchased one of the bootie vases, with flowers, and happened to be carrying it. What I encountered here was a coincidence.

And I was thinking, coincidences are so awesome!

And off I went, proceeding to the new wing. It was quicker to reach by going out a side door and crossing a courtyard. The night air was so chilly and sharp, I was jolted to alertness, all the way down to my bones.

I found the new wing as a wall of windows and a lighted interior where it looked like the gala for the opening was still going on, but with a different set of people, most of them in scrubs and whites.

The lobby was high and wide and expansive. The wing wasn't finished yet; it would soon be housing offices and a new outpatient clinic. When I stepped inside, I noticed a rack of brochures about its construction. I slipped one into my jacket pocket, feeling that reading it would be the price to pay for a meal.

The café tables and chairs set up for the gala were still in place. Several were occupied and it was easy to see who was who: doctors were with doctors, nurses with nurses, night clerks with night clerks. Two people from Housekeeping were at a table farthest away. I didn't see a familiar face. I headed for what was left of the buffet. It was mostly baked goods and *yay for that.*

There were still some paper plates, left by the caterers. I found some cheese chunks and grapes on an appetizer tray, which I could call my lunch. Then I loaded my plate with desserts.

I didn't want to sit at a table alone, nor did I want to go back outdoors before eating something. I knew I could have chosen any group to sit with. I knew I would have to be welcomed, new to the night shift as I still was. But I couldn't choose which one.

Which was fine. I didn't feel like taking part in conversations. I opted to wander around and find somewhere private.

Carefully clutching my plate, I crossed the lobby and stepped into a hallway lit by pale, milky night-lights. At the first doorway I looked into, I suddenly drew back, startled. The plate fell to the floor. I had lost the ability to hold it, the same as if my hands had turned to water.

The room was unfinished, still in a state of almost emptiness. Streetlight-type lamps from an adjacent parking lot gave just enough illumination through the bare windows, where the glass still had its manufacturer's stickers. I was seeing, on the wall I faced, a mural of a cloud.

A painter's canvas tarp was spread out like a carpet on bare, rough floorboards. The tarp was gray. Small, dry pools of white paint were everywhere on the cloth, as scattered snow would look on a patch of rocky ground, on a plateau that was situated some-where mountainous, like a roof at the top of the world.

The other walls were bare white panels of sheet rock. There was a hook on the unfinished ceiling, and suspended from it was a construction worker's powerful halogen light. The wattage must have been huge. When turned on, it would create a spotlight to be directed at the enormous cloud.

It was a perfect example of a cumulus, puffy and flat-bottomed, rising in rounded peaks, adrift against a background of pale-blue sky.

Frozen where I stood, I was aware that I should pick up the plate and the cake and tarts and cookies and cheese and grapes that slid off it. But I was incapable of cleaning up my own mess. My knees would not bend.

I couldn't think. I didn't even know what it meant to think a thought. When I finally felt unparalyzed, I walked away. No security cameras were in place; I checked.

I burst out of the first exit I came to, which opened to the medical center's interior.

Unlike the lawyer, in a maze of hallways, I knew where everything led. I moved swiftly, my head low, as if rushing to an emergency.

I ducked into the first ladies' room I reached. After washing and drying my hands, and deliberately not looking in the mirror, because I didn't want to know what my expression was like, I remembered the brochure.

A slip of paper, like an errata sheet, fell into the sink. I grabbed it eagerly, with the sense I was about to discover, somehow, an explanation. And then everything would be clear, would be logical.

As if I'd be given a message saying, "Dear Reverend, the cloud on the wall has nothing to do with the cloud of the lawyer!"

On the piece of paper was information about the room, which was intended to become a staffed, after-school play space for children of people who'd be employed in the new wing. No such thing existed in any other part of the medical center. It was a new-wing-office-people perk.

The painter of the mural had been called away to another project. The room as a whole would eventually contain sky murals of the four basic units in the twenty-four hours of a day. The cloud was afternoon. Morning would be a sunrise, twilight a sunset, night a glittering field of stars. The painter, it was hoped, would return as soon as possible. With the completion of the space delayed, please would everyone touring the new wing stay away from that area, as the painter had left behind some equipment?

Information about the painter was also given. She seemed to be very well known to people who know about such things. She had volunteered her work; someone close to her had once been treated at the medical center.

I crumpled the brochure and the paper into a wad, and dropped it in the wastebasket. What if I went to the lawyer's room and woke him? What if I told him there was something he needed to see?

What if he stood next to me in that doorway, looking into the room of the cloud, all of him, flesh and bones and his plain old eyes to see?

What would he say? And what might be broken inside him?

I thought of the little boy who couldn't imagine numbers going off into infinity, and gave up on math.

I thought of the man so awful to nurses and med-techs, but respectful to me, in my collar. I had not sat bedside with him to judge him. I thought of him as a boy who grew up to be able at last to *imagine.*

He was just like the baggage handler. He imagined his own heaven.

I had noted on the errata-like insert that the painter came from the state where the lawyer lived. Probably that wasn't a factor. But it might have been.

Maybe he had somehow known about this room. Maybe in his unit, he'd heard about the room. Maybe people were talking about it when he was in the ER, or post-surgery in a recovery room, lying there in the strange zone between awake and out of it, like a lying-down zombie, and the details went straight to the part of his brain that handles new information. His brain could have gone ahead and forwarded the information to his soul—I liked to think so.

Brains are so awesome!

"You didn't travel out of your body, because there's no such thing."

"I have evidence about your story."

Was I supposed to return to his room and say those words to him?

I was only his chaplain a little while. But I was his chaplain still. I could hear his voice, what it was like when he talked about joy, about Bach and Mozart not knowing anything about music, about himself becoming a pi, and what he now knew he could look forward to.

I imagined the lawyer looking at the unfinished room for children of office people. I imagined him facing the fact that, because of me, he would have to make a change to his story of his walk through the maze. I imagined him analyzing evidence. I imagined what would break inside him and always be broken.

"I reached the gate of infinity," he might say. "And it's a wall? That's it? Just some paint on a wall?"

Thirteen

As usual, the altar table was covered by a white linen cloth. In the center was a wide, white ceramic bowl in use as a planter, a gift from a small group of Quakers who had lost their meeting house in a fire, and used the chapel for free—my department just didn't tell the medical center about it. The Quakers made sure the bowl was always filled.

Tonight it was new-spring miniature hyacinths, pink and grape and light orange, their leaves firm and pale. Their sweet flowery smell rested lightly in the air.

On either side of the bowl were white candle lamps in small brass holders. The light of the filaments was almost gold, holding steady, unflickering. Sometimes I wish I'd kept count of how many times I had changed the batteries. I feel I have an inner monitor keeping track of when the lights are about to go out, the way other people might always know about moon phases, or what's going on with tides.

I have never told anyone I love this place as if it were a person. It felt good to say that verb.

"I love."

My hope to sit alone in a pew for a few minutes did not come true. I had been followed here, not that I had known it, until the resident appeared.

She sat down in the pew beside me. She was the person I'd spoken with about the lawyer.

Maybe she'd been heading for the chapel anyway. She was wearing fresh blue scrubs, no white coat. I could not recall her name. Her badge was obscured by the white towel draped over her shoulders. Since I'd seen her, she had showered. Her hair was shiny brown, like a chestnut shell, and it was still very damp, reaching down the sides of her face as straight as if she'd ironed it.

She was a little older than my age when I started out. But there was no comparison between her and the baby-chaplain me. This woman looked confident. She looked like, wherever she went, she would know how to do whatever was needed.

"I hate to waste time blow-drying," she said quietly. "I kind of got splattered by a patient a little while ago. But hey, it goes with the territory. You know what a great thing about nights is? You can walk around with a towel and no one cares."

There was a silence. She had a seniority among the residents, I recalled. She wanted to tell me something. Person to chaplain.

"The colors in here are nice," she said.

"I think so too."

"The walls, I mean, they're just right. But I never know what to call the color that's not yellow. I never know if it's mawve, or mohve."

She pronounced the *aw* and the *oh* distinctly. The sounds, to my ears, were weighted with the meaning of whatever she wasn't yet saying.

"I generally go with mahve," I said, holding back from mentioning that I was the one who chose the paint.

"I heard it was pretty dismal in here, but they renovated it. Were you around before they fixed it up?"

"I was."

"How do you like the night life?"

"I'm still getting used to it."

There was a long intake of breath. A getting ready. Physicians are terrible at talking about themselves when something is the matter with them personally.

But probably they say the same thing about chaplains.

"I'll be leaving here soon," said the resident.

Doctor Brown Hair, I'll call her.

"I've had an offer in a practice I'd been hoping for, so I don't think we'll have a chance to cross paths again. Do you mind, Reverend, if I say I need you to tell me we're speaking in confidence?"

"It doesn't need to be said. But yes, if you want to hear it, anything you tell me is mine only to know about."

"Thank you."

She had been staring straight ahead, but now she turned slightly toward me. What happened to her—what she did—was a story that she seemed to have gone over in her head many times, practicing the telling, perhaps wondering if it would ever be anywhere except inside herself.

"I've been hiding this in my soul," she said. "But all of a sudden, tonight, I just felt, I don't know why, I'd better come out with it."

It happened several months ago. December. She had a few days off and she was desperate to get away somewhere alone, somewhere not too far away, where she knew no one. She couldn't afford much of a vacation, even a brief one. So when her old college roommate offered her the use of a condo she owned with her husband, near a ski resort, she jumped at the chance.

Doctor Brown Hair was not a skier and had no interest in trying it out. But she was eager to visit the resort for its restaurant, spa, and heated pool. Her friend had given her a day pass and her own account information, as a Christmas present, and felt happy to do so because now she wouldn't have to think of a gift for someone who lived most of her life inside a hospital dressed in garments that looked like pajamas.

The morning was glorious: winter in a sunlit valley heaped with powdery snow, mountains wherever you looked, the temperature well above freezing. The resort had different levels depending on price, and she was bound for everything that was posh and most expensive.

Her spirits were as soaring as the peaks. She packed her carry-all with her bathing suit, pool gear, and sweats in case she felt like working out in their gym, a paperback novel for lounging poolside, and her iPod, loaded with two new albums she'd been looking forward to.

When she arrived at the resort, she checked in and decided to start at the juice bar, then have a massage and a facial, as the pool was being cleaned. She was just a few feet away from the entrance to the spa when the background music coming out softly, from speakers placed everywhere, came suddenly to a stop. It was chamber music stuff, lots of violins and cellos, where the cellos aren't ever depressing. You didn't realize you were listening to it until you weren't.

An announcement was being made.

There had been an accident on one of the slopes, involving multiple skiers. Was anyone present at the resort a doctor? Or any sort of medical professional? If so, please will you hasten to the foot of that slope and announce yourself to the gentleman in the orange parka with the vest that says he's the leader of the response team?

Doctor Brown Hair stood there clutching her bag. She had not zipped it closed. She stared down at the pair of her bathing caps. One was Lycra—that is, fabric. The other one, silicone, was a hood with a chin strap. She hadn't yet decided what she'd do in terms of laps. Before medical school, from the age of twelve, she had been a competitive swimmer. Her best stroke was the butterfly. She had hordes of trophies. But she'd been thinking about an easy time in the water that day; maybe she'd stick to aqua-jogging.

Then she zipped the bag shut. She could not remember how she signed herself in. She might have put an "MD" after her name. Just to do it. She was almost through with her residency. She had *earned* that title.

She found the lobby deserted. It was easy to look at the guest book on the counter. Hers was the last signature.

It was only her name, she saw. No telltale initials. She picked up a nearby pen and wrote her name again, this time as a checking-out. She put the time of the checkout earlier than it was. It looked as if she had only been in the resort a total of three minutes.

She exited by a side door and hurried to her car, in an area that wasn't near the slope of the accident. When she drove away, it was the same as if the announcement had never been made.

Setting her GPS for a town a few miles away, she realized she was remarkably calm. She was simply someone who had changed her mind about how she would spend her day. If there were ambulance and police sirens shattering the peace of that valley, she never heard them. She had blocked out sound.

"Too bad the resort didn't work out for me, when I was so looking forward to it," she was saying to herself.

The town turned out to be pleasantly old-fashioned. She shopped for new boots she put on in the store; her old ones were pretty worn down. She visited the local historical museum, then had lunch in a diner, treating herself to onion rings with her burger and two slices of banana cream pie. Then she discovered a movie theater, an independent one, another preservation, as if the year were in the nineteen-fifties; they were showing a double feature that afternoon. Both were movies she hadn't seen, because who has time for movies, doing what she does?

It was dusk when she drove back to the condo. At no time did she turn on her radio for news. She went to bed early and slept deeply until midmorning.

Before leaving the condo, she laundered and dried the sheets and remade the bed. She did not turn on the television. She did not go online. On her drive home, she plugged in her iPod. She took back roads and stopped a few times in coffee shops and restaurants that looked appealing.

Then she picked her life back up where she'd left off. Talking to her friend, she was full of gratitude, exclaiming how much she had loved her vacation. She described her day in the town, and only brought up the resort as an offhand comment. "Oh, I decided I wanted to be out in the world," she had said. Her friend didn't say anything about a ski accident, not then.

But about a week later, the friend phoned to say it was too bad

she hadn't been there: a skier approaching the base of an interme-
diate slope, at too fast a speed, had collided with another. That
impact caused yet another person to be injured, like a three-car
highway accident.

That slope is notorious for mishaps, the friend had declared.
People who belong on a beginner's trail are always overestimating
their abilities. And then they keep refusing to wear protective
headgear.

Doctor Brown Hair didn't question her friend about details of
the injuries or what came of the three skiers involved. It seemed
the resort was spending money to hush it up, not for the first time,
in fact. The official story was that something minor had taken
place.

The friend and her husband had just decided to put the condo
on the market. Did Doctor Brown Hair want one more trip there
before it was sold?

She did not. But after that conversation, she put her still-new
boots in a plastic bag and dropped the bag in a Goodwill dona-
tion box. She had found herself unable to look at them.

"You see, Reverend," she said, "what I'm talking about is, I have
no idea if I might have saved a life. I don't even know if a life was
lost. Or if I could've prevented an injury from being worse."

"I understand," I said.

"I don't think my friend would mention ski helmets if someone
hadn't been . . . well, you know what I mean."

I could almost hear the announcement breaking in to the background music. And the plea. Is anyone a doctor? Will you come
right away?

I wondered what I might have done in that position if a chaplain was being requested. I looked at the candle lamp to the right
of the hyacinths, then the one to the left. They were in sync. Their
batteries came from the same pack, put in at the same time, seconds apart. My first night on the night shift, I'd taken care of
that, even though I'd known there was still a lot of life in them. I

had wanted the feel of something extra, as if anything can shine brighter when batteries are brand new.

I said, "It seems to me you feel that you committed a crime."

She was taken by surprise, by that. Then she said, "Not a crime. A sin."

"In the last few years, how many hours a week have you been on duty?"

The physician laughed. It was a harsh, hard sound. "Who keeps track? I don't know."

"A rough estimate. An average."

"Seventy, maybe. Or ninety, I don't know."

"How long have your shifts been? Sometimes were they longer than the length of a day?"

"Oh, you know the answers to these questions, Reverend."

That was true. I once came upon an intern in an elevator, upright, leaned against the back wall, alone. He was fast asleep. A partially eaten sub was poking up from a pocket of his short white lab jacket. The car smelled like tuna salad. I didn't get on; I opted for the stairs. A little while later, I pushed for an elevator to leave the floor I'd gone to, and there he still was, with other people aboard, everyone quiet, leaving him be. Again I took the stairs, afraid that one more person pushing in might wake him.

I told this to Doctor Brown Hair, and she said, "In my first year, I sometimes thought I might die if I had to go into a room and see one more patient. But you've heard all this before. I can't be the first one talking like this to you."

"You're not," I said, leaning toward her, lightly touching the back of her hand as it rested on the seat of the pew. I patted that hand like I'd pat a dog.

I said, "Did you ever meet Bobo Boy? He used to work here."

"The therapy dog? Really odd looking? I haven't seen him around."

"He died, but that's not why I mentioned him. One day, he was led to the room of a woman who was beaten badly, viciously. She wasn't allowed visitors. Her assailant was a relative and he hadn't been found yet."

"Was that the woman whose husband hit her with a pipe?"

"No, it was a woman who was beaten with fists and kicks. She was unresponsive, and it seemed Bobo Boy might at least distract her. But he wouldn't go into that room. He lay down on the floor and just wouldn't. A doctor who thought he knew a lot about dogs picked him up to carry him in—the guy couldn't stand it that a command was being disobeyed. He felt Bobo Boy was committing the sin of dereliction of duty, which to be fair, is kind of accurate. I mean, with all his training and everything, and knowing his responsibilities. But Bobo yelped his head off and finally his handler took over. He'd had too much, the handler said. He'd just had too, too much. Even Jesus had to take a rest now and then, she told that doctor. What Bobo had to do was get out of the hospital and run around and be a dog and dig a hole or something."

"But it's not the same thing," Doctor Brown Hair said, almost cutting me off. "Animals don't sin. It's a human thing only. You'd never be able to convince me otherwise."

"Okay. Do you think he should have been ashamed of himself? He really did carry on. Imagine a dog screaming in a unit because he needed a break from his job."

"Why are you asking me that? Shouldn't you be telling me God forgives me?"

"I don't think this is about God. The forgive part, I mean."

Then I said, "Bobo Boy was great at his job. He had every right to be . . ."

"Human?"

"Something like that, yes."

She glanced at her watch. A new lightness came into her voice. "Oh, Reverend, I have to go! Good-night! I really have to rush!"

She turned in the doorway to wave to me. I sat there for a little while longer, listening to the stillness.

Bobo Boy never refused to enter the room of a patient. The woman who'd been beaten so badly had wanted to adopt him and bring him home with her. Once, he vomited on her blanket. She'd been secretly feeding him from her trays. It turned out he didn't do well with Jell-O—at least, not the type cut up in cubes and served on a plate in different flavors, orange and lime and cherry and lemon.

He didn't feel ashamed of that, I'd heard. The evidence of how he felt about puking was in the fact he next attempted to eat it. As dogs do. He had felt it was an injustice when his handler grabbed him and stopped him.

Once, I remembered, before we came under attack by the budget ax, and there was time in daylight to sit and talk, my boss, the Head, sat down with me to talk about ministers and being willing to say sometimes the things that need to be said, depending on a particular situation. He and I were recently chaplains together to the family of a young woman who had been placed on life support, after a shooting in a grocery store where a heavily armed former employee rushed in and opened fire. The young woman was one of half a dozen victims, five of whom had died where they had fallen. She was the manager of the produce section. She had shielded with her body another young woman, who was wearing a baby in a sling. She was a hero. Her family would not consider an end to life support. The woman would never come back to life.

A strange thing is that I have no memory of what I said to that family. It's gone. At the time I'd been double-shifting to cover for a colleague who was ill. I only remember that the Head, who knew the woman and the family, had left the talking to me. And I remember that the woman made that grocery store buy vegetables from local growers, and was a serious gardener herself.

The Head and I were with the woman's brother when it came time to let her go. The rest of the family had not felt able to watch it happen. I don't remember that either, only the fact I was there.

In that talk, the Head asked me if I had to learn to tell certain things at certain times to people I was ministering to—things that might not exactly be based on factual reality.

He seemed to be asking if I'd studied such a skill when I was being educated, being trained.

I had shaken my head no.

"So saying what has to be said is natural, like your curls?"

"It just comes to me, so I guess, yes," I had answered. "I would actually love to have straight hair."

And he had told me he hoped that I would always wake up in the morning to give myself the news all over again that I am blessed to be who I am, doing what I do how I do it. He was blessed to have hired me, he had told me, like he didn't know I knew I was not at the top of the list made by others on the hiring committee. I didn't do well in the interviews. The Head was the only one who loved the way I answered the question of, Why do I wear a collar, when most chaplains no longer do?

"I like to wear a collar the way I like to have a neck," I had said, quietly, gravely, calmly, telling the truth right down to the roots of its realness. If that had blown the job for me, I was willing to risk it.

Now I rose slowly to my feet in the wake of my lie to Doctor Brown Hair. I went to the pot of flowers and touched the soil to see if it needed watering. It didn't. The Quakers had that covered. I could not believe how glad it made me feel.

Fourteen

Here was the box of a room that's my office. Here was my desk, computer, and chair, one chair only, because this is a getaway for me. There in a corner was the metal filing cabinet containing extra collars and two changes of clothes, folded up as if meant for a suitcase.

Books were stacked somewhat untidily on a pair of wall shelves. The blinds on the one window were drawn, their slats closed tightly. I kept meaning to hang things on the walls, maybe some prints from a museum shop, but I'd never gotten around to it. When the poster of the beautiful weird animals went down in that waiting room, I'd tried to track it down so I could have it. I had failed.

It didn't feel strange to be here in the middle of the night alone, like a department of one. Someone had placed a carton of milk in our little fridge, and there was plenty left, so I didn't have to drink my coffee black. The fridge had nothing to eat. But in our supplies closet, as usual, there was a tin of excellent shortbread cookies—a regular contribution from a fellow chaplain who had not lost his job. He had learned to make them while attending seminary in Scotland.

On the shelf by the coffee machine, there used to be a crowd of mugs. Seeing how few were left made my chest cramp up, like the place in my chest where my heart is, was feeling some actual pain.

My own mug was a gift from the daughter of an elderly man I once sat with. It's big and wide, earthenware, simple, in a color of yellow-tan that looks like ground, powdery ginger.

The daughter had come looking for me one day. Having wandered into Pastoral Care, she found me drinking afternoon tea from a paper cup. I'd never remembered to bring in a real one.

Please would the curly-gingery-haired chaplain sit for a while with her dad?

The elderly man had asked for me in exactly that way. I had only visited him briefly before. He had not been open to a talk with a member of the clergy.

The daughter had been staying closely by him, knowing how sick he was. But she'd slipped away to go home for a rest. Her father did not start acting weirdly until after she'd left the hospital. Now that she'd been summoned back, she was alarmed.

I suddenly remembered all of this. What had happened.

Maybe, at the time, I didn't believe it, as if the event took place in a dream. Afterward I never thought about it again. Until now.

It was a windy day, with gusts blowing almost as fiercely and wildly as a hurricane. I found the old man crying. But it wasn't because he'd been left alone.

His face was quite thin, his cheekbones pronounced, to the point of a gauntness that was hard to look at. Anyone would be able to tell that a fleshy and vibrant robustness had once been there. His bed had been cranked up a little, so that he wasn't lying flat. The coverings had been pulled to the top of his chest and tucked fairly tightly below the mattress, with his arms inside, in a sort of swaddling.

The walls of that room were a soft beige. The evidence of what he'd been up to was on the wall behind his bed, a few inches beyond the frame: a gash in the paint, surrounded by tiny nicks and scratches. The wall itself had not been penetrated, just chipped at.

The old man had been losing the ability to sip water. An aide who was feeding him ice chips had briefly gone out of the room, leaving behind, on his bed table, the cup of ice and the spoon. The ice, he didn't bother with, but he had taken the spoon in hand. He had managed to turn himself so he was facing the wall. He had attacked it, holding the round part of the spoon as a handle.

When the aide returned, she had to summon help. The old man's burst of strength was a surprise, especially when he put up so much resistance. He didn't want to be stopped. He didn't want that spoon taken away from him.

Three staffers formed a team to get him settled down again. Before this, he'd been quiet, even subdued. He had shown no signs of dementia. He had not seemed capable of any act of destruction whatsoever.

The attending physician hadn't wanted to sedate him any more than he was medicated already.

When resisting the staffers, the old man had shrieked and wailed, but refused to speak. He began to sob loudly as he was being tucked in, but when I entered his room, he went silent. He refused to accept any more ice. The aide at his side was dabbing his cheeks with a tissue. Silently, his tears were streaming down his face like water from a faucet that could not be turned all the way off.

Meanwhile the wind was slamming against the building, against the windows. The aide left the room, with the ice and the spoon. I sat down at the edge of his bed, with the sense that something was happening that had never happened to me before.

He was talking to me.

Not in words. Not with a look, as his expression was blank, impassive. He seemed neither glad nor disapproving to see that I had come. Yet all the ordinary space that exists between two people who don't know each other had somehow instantly dissolved.

The daughter hovered in the background, witnessing, saying nothing.

This man had not been destructive. He had not been trying to damage the wall. He had been trying to create an escape.

His window drapes were closed, cutting off the window as a way out for his soul. He knew he was just a little while away from the end of his life. He was terrified.

Not of dying. Of his soul being trapped.

I happened to have a pen in my pocket. I took it out. The old man, I realized, wanted me to take up with the wall where he had left off.

How can a soul speak to another soul?

I couldn't explain it.

I gripped the pen as if holding a knife. I showed him that I was willing to cut a hole for him in that wall, as if, on the other side, there'd be open air, not the room of some other patient. I knew that what he wanted was a way out for his soul.

He told me that.

His bed wasn't near the windows. Probably if it were, he might have asked for a window to be opened for him. He wasn't scared about the hard-blowing wind. He didn't want to escape it. He wanted to join it.

The last thing he looked at was my hand, wielding the tool of the pen, as I rose to face the wall, ready to carry on the attack.

His eyes closed when I was up on my feet beyond his field of vision. He was lying there picturing the hole expanding. I had made a delusion. I had done my job.

In the moments after he died, I touched my fingers to his face, where his skin was still damp from tears. I believe he had imagined the powerful wind as the breath of God, and he was ready to feel that his soul was breaking loose, as a strong, big bird would firm itself up to rise.

I believed so because he told me that too.

Something in my brain had blocked that day. Or had tried to blot the memory out, because things need to have explanations or they didn't really happen.

Something like that. And now I was sitting at my desk, hands on my mug. I had limited myself to four shortbread cookies. The tin had been full. When my shift drew near to a close, should I return to the room of the lawyer?

I was being paged. Something had happened. *All hands on deck.*

Fifteen

It was a winter of heavy snowfalls. At a factory warehouse turned into a discounted, surplus, general merchandise retail outlet, the snow that piled over and over on the flat roof was left to melt. The roof and its buttresses could pass a building inspection, but had never been structurally sound enough to withstand a lot of stress.

The store was under new management. In previous years, following a snow- or rainstorm, day laborers were hired to go up on the roof with shovels or push brooms. This was the first year those chores were eliminated from the budget. Also eliminated was the job of the maintenance foreman, leaving the care of the building to some guys who were mostly still teenagers, hired at minimum wage, and basically their own supervisors.

The disaster had been waiting to happen. It would not have been a disaster in human terms if this weren't the night of what the store called its first-ever Spring Midnight Madness clearance sale.

The doors were reopened at midnight. From then until dawn, prices were slashed considerably, and there were hourly specials in all departments, as well as raffles, free coffee and donuts, and giveaways of spring things such as Easter baskets and equipment for outdoor grilling. The sale was promoted intensely. The new managers had even rented billboards on well-traveled smaller highways.

When the roof collapsed, some three hundred people were inside, and nearly half that number in the parking lot, where food-truck vendors, subsidized by the store, were charging next to nothing for tacos, chili dogs, soft-whip ice cream, fried dough.

The implosion came with a warning. In the central area of the store, loose debris began raining down, sending shoppers scurrying, so that the worst section of the collapse did not entrap anyone.

The first 911 callers reported that the building might have been bombed, which meant there was a fast, massive police and rescue response.

Most of the victims were taken to two hospitals nearer the scene. The medical center was third in line, and still, as more ambulances arrived, the ER and its waiting room were packed, and in a state of chaos that would have been actual chaos if not so well controlled.

By the time I arrived in the area of the ER, I saw that two clergy people were already there. I spotted a Congregational minister who frequently made night visits to members of his parish who were very sick, sleepless patients knowing they could phone him in the middle of the night—he was famous for being an insomniac. And my own colleague was here—yes, the guy of the cookies, waving at me. I remembered he was also a chaplain of the fire department.

We spoke briefly. He was just stopping by. He was on his way to the scene, then back to bed. Hang in there!

Then I saw a rabbi I know, on her way to the ambulance entrance. For the first time I'd been summoned to a crisis, I didn't know what to do with myself.

Then someone was tugging at my arm. A woman in a coat and head scarf that were heavily dusted from plaster had something to tell me. She looked dazed, but not injured. She told me that she'd ventured to a hallway just beyond the ER, looking for someone to tell her it would be okay if she went home, since she'd been brought in accidentally. She had seen an old woman alone on a gurney back there. It seemed to her that someone needed to be with that person. She had figured that, wearing a collar, I would want to know.

A man was walking by us. He had on a denim jacket soaked red all over the front. He was glassy-eyed, in shock. But he paused for a moment.

"Good evening, Reverend," he said. "This here blood isn't mine. There was kind of some trouble with sharp edges of things, I think."

A nurse appeared, took hold of him, led him away.

"She's very, very old," added the woman talking to me. "I think she had a stroke. I've seen them before."

I thanked her. Taking a deep breath, I set myself in motion.

The old woman in the out-of-the-way little corridor, lying on a gurney, had a sheet pulled up to her waist, and yes, she was alone. There wasn't a hospital bracelet on her wrist—she hadn't been processed. She appeared to be somewhere in her late eighties or early nineties.

Her pale-blue eyes had the sharpness and clarity of a bird's. She looked at me with a wary suspicion.

I thought of the librarian. The nightgown of this woman was a flowery, flannel one, round in the collar with a fringe of lace. How many very old, very alone women had I been chaplain to, with the same garment or some small variation? Many.

At the foot of the gurney was a pink quilted bathrobe.

"Hi. I'm a chaplain here. Are you able to speak? Can you tell me something about yourself?"

The stroke appeared to have been fairly minor. But the old woman's mouth showed that it had not yet worn off. One corner of her mouth went upward a little, as if pulled by an invisible string. She looked frozen in half of a smile, or half of a grimace. She did not seem to be in pain.

Her reply was mumbly: the guttural voice of anyone under Novocain in a dentist's chair. But she was getting it across to me that she didn't want to be here. She had been brought against her will, and didn't she have the right to decide herself if she wanted treatment in a hospital? Where she lived was no great place, but it was home to her. She was ninety-one. At her age, did she not have the right to say no to being in a hospital?

Slowly, her face showing signs of strain, she lifted both arms a couple of inches, indicating she was not in paralysis.

I smiled at her warmly. Yes, I was saying with a nod. There are such things as rights.

"I'll be back in a minute. I promise," I said.

The first nurse who wasn't too busy to speak with me was not an ER nurse. She'd been pressed into service from a unit where patients are not in a state of consciousness—and as a longtime coma care person, she was overwhelmed by what she viewed as uncontrolled mayhem. She welcomed the chance to turn away for a few moments from the collapse victims.

The old woman's name was Mrs. Marjorie Copp. She was a widow and had lived for many years in a senior care facility I knew of as a place that's always understaffed and overcrowded.

An ambulance was called when a staffer observed her with symptoms of a stroke. She was treated briefly by an ER physician who wanted her admitted as an inpatient for observation and various tests. It seemed the stroke was not her first. The danger was big: there could be another one on the way, a major one. The brain of Mrs. Copp could have been holding a time bomb in need of defusing.

She was not in the medical center's computer system. A call had been made to her facility, to gather some information. But the call went to voice mail and so far had not been returned. Mrs. Copp herself had not been able or willing to answer questions about her background and health. She had arrived with no insurance card, no forms about treatment, no medical proxy, no anything. Probably soon, someone would figure out how to get her admittance taken care of. Of course she couldn't stay in this hall indefinitely.

"But she might not want to be admitted," I said.

The nurse looked at me in a very critical manner, as if saying, "You have got to be kidding me."

Her uniform was nursing whites, pristine. She was out of her element, and tense and tired, and she might have been harboring personal disappointments and bitterness she couldn't stop from slipping into her job. Her voice took on a cold, disapproving tone as she shared with me her belief that Mrs. Copp was in a state of dementia.

In an effort to reach out to her, the nurse had addressed the old woman as Marge instead of Marjorie.

"She got pretty cross with me. And she asked me if I thought she looked like someone with blue hair, and a beehive," said the nurse.

"Blue hair?"

"That's what she said. And *bees.*"

"Hang on," I said. "That's from television. That's Marge Simpson. She might have meant she doesn't like that nickname. You know what I'm talking about? The show? The cartoon? Marge Simpson's hair is a blue beehive?"

The nurse did not seem to think I might be right in making that connection.

"It's dementia," she said. "Marge also swore to me she saw a dog. Right here. Believe me, there wasn't one."

I did not let on my reaction to that. "A dog? Did she say what it looked like?"

"She didn't, just that it was strange."

"Strange like unfamiliar to her? Or strange like it was weird looking?"

"She wasn't talking about a real dog, Reverend. You know how it is with these cases. They lose their bearings, they get angry. They think they're the ones that are sane and everyone else is out of it. Don't you think you should be sticking to your own job?"

I let the sting of that question linger in the air. I wasn't taking it personally.

"I'm sorry," the nurse said. "I didn't want to sound mean. I do feel bad for that old lady. I'm only trying to say she's not the right judge for her care. Excuse me now, I have to get back to the disaster people."

Back I went to the little hall. Mrs. Copp was staring up at a lighting fixture in the ceiling. The effects of the stroke had worn off a little bit more. Her mouth was relaxing, settling back to its own shape. She was grasping the top of the sheet in its fold at her waistline. Her hands were fisted. The knobs of her knuckles were prominent, like a miniature set of ridgetops. The backs of her hands were blue-veined, skin-shiny, and almost translucent.

Those hands looked delicate, breakable, *old*.

"Hi, again," I said.

She tugged at the sheet, so that it came loose from the end of the gurney. Her feet were in clean white socks. Her bathrobe was hanging off the edge. It was the same shade of pink as cotton candy.

"Please," she said. "I want to sit up."

I held out my arm for Mrs. Copp to use like a pull-up bar. She managed to raise herself, and as she did, a smell of urine came wafting my way. The old woman seemed not to be aware of it.

She was quite small, even tiny. Her white hair was straight and wispy-thin, in short, slightly uneven bangs, as if she had trimmed them herself, perhaps without looking in a mirror, perhaps with a hand that had trembled.

Her mouth was toothless. When she reached toward the underside of her pillow, I had no idea what she meant to do, until she produced the set of her dentures.

She'd been hiding her teeth. Maybe they were in her mouth when the ambulance people came into her room to take her away. Maybe she'd been allowed to retrieve them from a glass of water. In the ER, she might have concealed them, out of anxiety they'd be taken away from her.

She was able to insert her teeth without looking like the effort caused her discomfort. At once, as soon as she opened her mouth to speak again, the top plate loosened and slipped, in a whisper of a click as it landed on the lower.

So she inserted a thumb into her mouth to hold the plate in place. She was not embarrassed or apologetic about it. This was her body. It was just doing what it was doing.

The corner of her mouth that wasn't locked anymore formed an actual smile. But now she had to talk around her thumb.

She had a sense of humor, this lady. I was about to wish with all my heart I had a tube of teeth adhesive in a pocket of my jacket, placed there for just this occasion.

"Should I . . . call . . . you . . . my chap . . . lain?"

"Yes. That's what I am," I answered.

"Then, Chap . . . lain . . . I must ask . . . you . . . impor . . . tant . . . ques . . . shun."

"What is it, Mrs. Copp?"

"Got . . . goop?"

She said it exactly like the "got milk?" in the famous milk commercials. I felt myself melting with tenderness for this person, thumb in her mouth, sitting there showing me what her soul was like.

"I don't have goop but I can find you some," I said.

Mrs. Copp shook her head. She didn't want me leaving her side again.

"I want," she said, "a . . . taxi. Get out . . . of here. I can . . . pay."

I let that go by for the moment.

"I'm wondering, Mrs. Copp, if there might be something to take care of before we talk about anything else. It seems to me you might be dealing with some, you know, wetness. I wonder if we should think about finding you something else to wear. I bet I could rustle something up."

"Gown."

"You mean your nightgown?"

"Not wet."

I didn't want to make a fuss about the odor. It was true that I had seen no evidence of wetness. I'd been assuming it.

"Got diaper. Soo . . . per . . . preem . . . ium," said Mrs. Copp, a little proudly. "Trank . . . quill . . . ah . . . tee."

She was wearing a diaper! The brand was Tranquility!

I gave her a nod. "Would you like me to arrange for a clean one?"

No. She wanted nothing from the hospital. She held out her hand for her robe, and I passed it to her.

"Clean things can be taken care of later. Can I help you put this on, Mrs. Copp?"

"Marge," the old woman said. "Call me . . . Marge."

"Oh, but I heard from the nurse you spoke with that you don't like to be called that."

"I don't like . . . that show, Chap . . . lain. But right now I . . . feel I am a . . . car . . . toooon."

"You are *not* a cartoon, Mrs. Copp."

"Will you . . . help me?"

"I understand that you don't want to be a patient in a bed here," I said. "But there are things that need to happen. It's complicated because everyone's so busy. The thing is, your body went through some trouble and it's reasonable for the doctor to be concerned about you. I've been told they're waiting for information from your residence. I promise you I'll stick by you."

That was as far as I got before we were interrupted.

An orderly in gold-colored scrubs was approaching. He was young, burly, and sort of military in his bearing. His head was shaved except for a short patch on top. His forearms were covered with intricate spiderworks of tattoos, the lines and squiggles all black, all stark against the whiteness of his skin. Why couldn't someone have come along I knew?

The robe in Mrs. Copp's hands looked like something being formed into a weapon. She was bunching it up, raising it. She appeared ready to throw it at this man. I could not tell which was more powerful in her expression: anger or fear. She seemed to understand he had arrived to take her out of the hall.

"Whoa," said the orderly. "I'm your friend."

He turned to me, his nostrils flaring. He was smelling the odor of urine.

"Is this the dementia patient? Is she unstable? I'm supposed to ask, like, if she needs to be secured."

Perhaps he was new. Perhaps in his training, no one told him not to speak of a patient as if the patient isn't right there.

"Mrs. Copp," I said, "please tell him what you told me, about being admitted."

The old woman refused to speak. It was the same as if she were deaf.

Then he addressed her directly, slowly, in a softer voice. He could have been an adult trying to reason with a rowdy, unpredictable child he was determined to be gentle with.

"I'm taking you for a ride, dear, seeing as how the bed you're sitting on has wheels. You and I are going to a room and we'll get you settled in. Then they'll be taking you to another one, to run some little tests. They won't hurt one bit."

"Stop a minute here," I said. "She hasn't consented to treatment. Or to being admitted. Did her nursing home come through with information?"

"I don't know about that," the orderly answered. "You work here?"

My name badge was right there on my jacket. I pointed to it.

"I'm in the chaplaincy."

"So you're not a next of kin or something."

"It doesn't matter," I said.

"Well, she's down for admission. Looks to me it's not open to debate. She's booked for a CT, blood, the whole works."

"Please," I said, "will you find out if any information came in? And I know Mrs. Copp wants to speak to the physician who examined her."

Reluctantly, he went back to the ER, and Mrs. Copp lifted one hand from the clutch of her robe, to prop up her top plate again.

"Go . . . home, Chaplain. No . . . cat."

"A CAT scan, do you mean? You've had one before?"

A nod, two nods.

"I don't think you've been a patient here before."

"An . . . other hos . . . pital. But all are . . . the same. And no . . . cath."

It was not a repetition of "cat." She saw my confusion.

"Cath is when . . . can't go to . . . bathroom. For the lab . . . tech . . . ni . . . shun."

"A catheter? Mrs. Copp, are you talking about something that was done to you?"

"Sample. Couldn't . . . go. They said . . . have to give . . . sample."

"Did you have urine drawn with a catheter? Is that what you're telling me?"

"They put it . . . in me. A tube. You know? *Way in.* You know . . . what I mean?"

"I do. I do know what you mean. I promise you, it won't be done to you again."

"It hurt."

"Yes. It would have."

"Bad."

"No one is going to hurt you," I said.

I reached for the robe, intending to help Mrs. Copp put it on. But she was holding it with a tight grip. I realized that she had taken a turn to a dark place in her memory. Her top plate of teeth had slipped again. A hardness came over her face, like a new paralysis.

Whatever she was feeling was exhausting her, on top of the aftermath of her stroke. She had lost the strength to sit upright. She let herself sink back, her head landing on the pillow as if her whole body had fallen lengthwise.

I had made a mistake in moving for the robe. She had thought I meant to take it away from her, like robbing her. She thought I couldn't be trusted.

What to say? What to say? What to say?

"Mrs. Copp? Will you tell me about the dog you saw?"

She relaxed immediately. I was back in her graces. Her thumb was in her mouth again. "Want dog . . . want him . . . to come back."

"Can you tell me what he looks like?"

"Boxer. He's . . . spes . . . shell. He's big."

A big boxer?

The ghost of Bobo Boy could not by any stretch of the imagination resemble such a dog. I felt silly for thinking that way.

"Special how, Mrs. Copp?"

"He can . . . be . . . in . . . visible."

"But you saw him, this boxer?"

That's when we heard another person in the hall. A physician I knew slightly was passing by, speaking into his phone, walking in long strides. He wore a long white coat, unbuttoned, billowing out around him.

The seizure might have been gathering all along, its power slowly building. It began to happen in the split second before it was clear that the physician took no notice of Mrs. Copp. He turned the corner, vanished.

There was a gasp, like a swallow of too much air. The head on the pillow tipped upward, eyes opening wide, wider. The old woman's hands flailed at the air, briefly, then came to a rest at her sides.

A stiffness went through Mrs. Copp's body. Her mouth opened wide. Her top plate of teeth jutted forward, like a partly open drawer. Swiftly, reflexively, as if I'd handled someone's teeth many times, I removed that top one, then the bottom, which had fully come loose.

I looked at the pink fragility of the old woman's mouth, toothless like a bird's. I remembered reading somewhere that birds became birds only when their ancestors stopped having teeth. It was the lightness of their mouths that let them be airborne. It wasn't just about growing wings.

"It's all right," I whispered. "I know you can hear me. I know it's all right."

There was no way for her to answer the questions I wasn't asking. Do you want me to call a code on you? Do you want me to bring people running? Do you want to be hooked to equipment, to have needles put into your skin, to let powerful drugs course into you, to perhaps have your heart shocked with voltage from paddles? To have a tube put into your throat, old as you are, mute as you are right now? Do you want to be taken upstairs in an elevator and *kept alive*?

"Go in peace," I whispered. "All is well."

With the dentures in my hand, I bowed, to be closer to the face so strangely tilted, the eyes looking up at the light. I touched the side of my face to that other one, feeling with my own cheek the old, thin, well-worn skin.

Then I let out my own breath. I hadn't realized I was holding it in, as if I had jumped in a dive, into deep, dark water. My heart had fisted up in my chest, but now it was beating again.

I picked up the pink bathrobe. I placed the dentures in one of the pockets. I never had the chance to ask what was holy to her. But I think she would have answered, "My own self."

In a moment, after calling out an alarm, I'll be speaking to the gold-scrubs orderly, ER people, the nurse who was only here because a roof had collapsed. The orderly will turn his head, looking away from me, but not before I see his eyes pool up. I will learn he's new. I will slip my hand into his: a chaplain to a young man seeing his first death.

And again I'll be paged.

Sixteen

It shouldn't have hurt but it did. It really hurt.

You're not a priest. You take off that collar, you hear me?

The man in the bed, age sixty, had been injured by debris in the roof collapse. When he asked for a chaplain, he might have been confused about which hospital he'd been brought to.

No religious affiliation was listed on his intake forms, which anyway, given the circumstances, were incomplete. He was being stabilized, and possibly would need surgery.

He had been shopping at the store on his own. Calls to his wife at home had not been answered. He had given the information that their habit was to turn off the ringer when they retired for the night. He had not given any other contact names or numbers.

Newly an inpatient, he found himself in a zone of lonely strangeness. No one in his life knew where he was, or what happened to him. Apparently he had slipped out of bed and gone out to the sale as a secret.

He ran a small masonry business. After years of never having the time or inclination to build a patio behind his house, he had decided to do so. Money was tight in his family. He had seen a commercial that the store was offering wrought iron patio furniture at a price for a whole set you would normally pay for just one chair.

Out he had ventured in his pickup, planning to hide the furniture under covers in his garage, which his wife almost never went into. He meant the whole thing as a surprise. If he had stayed outdoors on the lot, where the furniture was, he would not have been a victim. But he'd gone in because they said on the loudspeaker they were giving away free barbecue equipment. Also, the cushions for the chairs were inside.

He was revived at the scene by paramedics, after being found unconscious.

In the medical center, reports were coming in about victims knocked down and hurt by a rush of shoppers acting in what sounded like a stampede. The man had refused to tell his nurses how his serious bruising and damage occurred. Although he'd been sedated, he was waging a battle against falling asleep, and he was winning.

He wanted a chaplain to talk to him about Jesus and the parable of the Good Samaritan. He'd been specific about it to one of his nurses, like he was sending out a work order for the chaplain to contemplate on the way to his room.

He had worked as a mason all his life, he had said, and never once, until now, had he experienced the feeling that his soul, inside him, was as heavy as stones he had lifted and held. His nurse had felt he was telling her this to put a special emphasis on his need for spiritual help, maybe in case the chaplain was busy with other patients.

He had wanted to flag his work order as an emergency.

He was a man of faith, he'd said.

His religion meant everything to him, he'd said.

The consensus in his unit was that, trying to escape the collapse, he fell, or he was pushed. His location was near an exit. He had not been hidden under rubble. Most of his injuries would fit a theory of being trampled. He must have huddled on the floor as an obstacle, perhaps holding out his hand for help, expecting someone in the crowd to stop and help him.

The Gospel of Luke was in my mind as I hurried to his side. It had moved me deeply to know that the mason was reaching out for comfort this way. I did not have a Bible but I didn't need New Testament text in front of me. I could either recite the story, or list off the elements and then talk about it.

Jesus is approached by a lawyer. His question is, How does one gain eternal life?

And the story of the beauty and the power of compassion follows, with its solid and solemn truth. There is kindness. There is hope. There is faith. There is the figure of the Samaritan, a giant in the world of all stories, without a name of his own, not that he needs one. He becomes his own actions.

A certain man went out one day and he was badly wounded.

It all begins with a lawyer, I was planning to say, knowing how aware I'd be that in another part of the hospital, the lawyer of the cloud was hours away from his release.

Reaching the mason's doorway, I steeled myself to get ready, glad that I'd been given a heads-up on his appearance, his condition. The room was dusky, the shape in the bed quite still. His head was bandaged. I stepped toward the foot of the bed so he didn't have to turn his head to see me.

What part of me did he see first? My hair, the hair of a woman? My chest inside my jacket, and the swell of a woman's breasts? My neck, bearing a white collar?

From the expression on his face as he stared at me, I had the thought that if he had held an object in his hand, and had the ability to throw it, he would throw it at me, like Mrs. Copp with her bunched-up nightgown.

But I felt that a weapon in his hands would not be soft. He might have been, all along, a violent man, the violence perhaps always just under his surface. I saw that I outraged him. I was not what he had ordered.

"You're not a priest. You take off that collar, you hear me?"

The weakness of his physical self and the effects of the drugs he'd been given did not diminish the intensity of his voice, bursting all around me. I considered for a moment trying to speak with him anyway—but two nurses came running in.

It was personal. I didn't want it to be, but it was.

"We're sorry, we're sorry," murmured those nurses. The bellowing voice had stunned them. They looked like they'd been wounded too. But their job was taking care of the patient, not taking care of me.

I entered a small waiting room at the end of that hall and there I sat, in the center of an upholstered sofa, feet flat on the floor, arms crossed at my chest like I was hugging myself: the chaplain who didn't minister to a man who had claimed his soul was heavy like stone.

I leaned back. The sofa was far from new. The cushions were saggy, dented from the weight of many who were here before me. I was too tired to cry, I felt, even though I'd tanked up on coffee in my office.

Then there was my phone. A text.

"I got up to pee. You there? You okay?"

My sister.

"I'm here," I typed. "Taking a break. Just have a minute."

"Well I got a feeling something's wrong."

"Don't worry, I'm fine."

"I have a checkup next week. Tests & stuff."

"Here?"

"Yeah. I hate them so much."

"I know. I'll come with you."

"Thanks, got it for early a.m. when you're post shift & you'll be wiped but I'll treat coffee."

"Just coffee?"

"All right a whole breakfast. Don't tell anyone about the appt."

"I won't."

"I'm sure it'll be fine."

"Me too!"

"Remember that day you faked you passed out, the soccer tryouts?"

I never know what memory she'll pull out, waving it around like a flag. That particular one is a sore spot, even though it happened almost thirty years ago. But that's the thing about a family. The past is never the past. It just all keeps on being right there.

"I do remember that day," I typed.

"Good. I was just thinking about it. I want you to know I forgive you."

"Wait. YOU forgive ME?"

"That's right. And guess what. My gym's having a special for new members. I'm thinking, I'll cover the cost. Don't you think it's time?"

She never gives up on this subject. Join my gym, work out!

"No thanks."

"You need exercise."

"I get it. Plenty."

"You don't. You'll turn into a human dumpling."

"Got to go."

"You're mad."

"I'm not."

"Did someone just die?"

"Don't want to talk about it."

"Who was it?"

"A woman. Old. I'm sad."

"Were you with her?"

"Yeah."

"She was lucky to have you and that's a fact. Have a good rest of your shift. Bye!"

Getting mad at her is the same as being mad about a change in the weather and expecting it to change for the better, just because of a feeling. Last year, when her mammogram showed something that could be serious, I was the only person she told.

She made me promise that, if she were dying, before she ever had the chance to be amazing at being elderly, I would become her chaplain and sit with her. My one duty would be to keep away anyone who might come into her room and try to cheer her up. She would want to use the last of her energy to stay mad that she was losing her energy.

The scare wasn't cancer. But she was still afraid. My big sister. And what if she were here, and she knew how the mason hurt me? She might not care about his injuries and what he'd been through.

Yet she had texted that moment, giving me her presence.

And a memory.

It was a Saturday morning, spring, newly spring, like now, and I had locked myself in a stall, in a row of several porta-potties along the edge of a soccer field.

And there was my sister, thumping the side.

It was registration day for the little-kid teams. I hadn't known that. I had thought I was being dragged to the field to be a spectator, same as usual. I would lie down on the grass and look up, up, always up. I would think my fairy would stir in me if I kept watching clouds go by.

I would believe I could feel the earth below me, turning and tilted, revolving in its orbit, slowly, slowly through space. "Me and my soul are riding our planet," I would say, as if I had draped myself over a giant ball, suspended in the sky.

I thought that staring at clouds might be magical, might bring that other thing. I never felt that running through a soccer field kicking a ball would quite manage to do it.

Probably my sister was babysitting me that morning. Then I realized I wasn't brought here to watch her play, or watch a team she was coaching.

The toilet stall stank of chemicals and a trash bin that had no lid. I had locked the door anyway.

"Get out of there right now!"

Thump, went those hands on the side. Then *thump* even more on the front.

My sister was a giant then. If I didn't come out, she was going to tip over that stall.

I came out. I felt I'd been captured. I knew that all you had to do to qualify for a team was run down the field and not die. I knew what dying was.

I cooperated. When I reached the halfway point, I let myself drop, in a slowly sinking way, so it wouldn't look as if I'd tripped on my own feet and fallen.

I lay very still, my eyes closed. The people in charge of the registration believed I was briefly unconscious, and needed to be taken to a hospital.

My sister talked them out of calling an ambulance. She carried me to the car, but as soon as we were out of sight, she stopped hurrying. She knew exactly what I'd done, but only after she'd reached my side on the field.

She set me down. She didn't do so roughly. Another type of sister might have.

"You scared me right down to my soul," she said. "You scared me so bad, I think you almost broke it."

I forgot she had tricked me into trying out for soccer. I felt a terrible chill go through me, as if I weren't wearing clothes, as if a cold wind entered me, through my skin.

I will never forget what it was like to find out what I knew I could never unlearn.

A soul can be broken?

Seventeen

"You have to go to your office."

"I was just there."

"Go back. Something's coming."

I was texting with my boss, the Head. He was up because the strangeness of this night had reached into other places—but really, two wailing, teething babies were making sure no one in his house stayed asleep.

One of his daughters was the mother of those twins. They were visiting. He was trying to balance being a good dad and grandfather with the part of himself that wanted to urge them to stay in a hotel, or go to a hotel himself.

He's a Unitarian minister and he came to hospital chaplaincy after years on United Nations missions around the world. His own life had been seriously in danger when he became ill with a virus; the damage will never go fully away. He walks with a cane. He's in his fifties, but already has the beginnings of an old man's stoop.

The cuts to our department felt to him like a battle he was responsible for losing. He was still amazed he was a peaceable man talking about our jobs in terms of war.

"I heard about the roof," he texted. "How are you doing?"

"One D," I answered, in our shorthand. "Not from the roof. Someone from a nursing home."

"Rough night."

"Yeah."

"I ordered you a pizza."

"You what?"

"From the all-night place."

"Well great, thanks, how come?"

"To be honest, I don't know. But it popped into my head you might be hungry, so go to your office for the delivery."

"What kind of pizza?"

"Sorry to say, just plain, but extra cheese. They claimed they're out of toppings. That's hard to believe, but I didn't argue. Must go. I promise we'll start rotating shifts soon. Most grateful to you. B says hi. Over and out!"

B is the Head's daughter. When she married, it was in the chapel, the first thing to go on when the renovations were done. That had been a good day. I hadn't minded it when everyone kept telling me, "You're next."

No one knew the almost-ness of *me, married*.

I never had the chance to say these words to anyone: "I'd like you to meet the man I'm in love with."

Don't think about that.

But there it was, coming over me, like a sort of attack. The hurt of it, all over again. The surprise of it. The Green Man. His smell. His fingernails, crusted inside with plant dirt.

His body, fitting itself against me.

His laugh. His work boots.

What I almost did. What I still felt so ashamed of.

He moved away somewhere unknown, I now knew.

His spacious, airy, light-filled apartment was at the top of an old stone building, four stories high, converted from a long-ago trade school. The roof was flat. The trapdoor in the ceiling of his bedroom had been sealed, but he worked on it, opened it up, bought a stepladder. I had told him I wanted to be up on the roof with him and look at the sky. I had been happy.

He had almost been taken to meet my family. All of them at once.

Just throw him into it, I had thought. For some holiday. Not say ahead of time I'd be bringing someone.

He grew up an only child. His parents were quiet people, polite, their voices always moving along one straight line, as if softly marching. I had met them. I had told him I felt they were very reserved with me. But he said they were like that all the time.

I advised him to wear earplugs whenever I got around to bringing him to the house I grew up in. No one would notice. He wore his hair past his ears, unlike every male I'm related to.

The parking lot next to his building was for residents only. There was a pole for a gate, a card reader to stick a card into.

This was when I was still on the day shift. I had not believed we'd broken up. I had been ready to do something I felt powerless to stop myself from doing. I had been ready to forgive him for something he would not say he was sorry for—and tell him he was right about something I knew was wrong.

It was early in the morning. I had left my own apartment more than an hour ahead of my shift. To go and see him. I knew he'd be home. I knew he'd let me in when I buzzed.

He'd been right that night, and I was in love with him. Something like that. I hadn't planned the words exactly. I would speak into the speaker.

He had taken back my keys to his building. What I hadn't known that morning was that my card to get into the parking lot had been invalidated.

I pulled up to the pole, and had to back out into traffic. When someone blared a horn at me, I thought he'd appear in one of his windows, like he'd guessed I was there.

His neighborhood had highly restrictive on-street parking. All the possible places to park were filled. Yet I drove around and around his block, waiting, hoping for a spot to open up. I was nervous about it; I'm terrible at parallel parking.

At a red light, I phoned him, even though he had not responded to any of my other calls. His voice mail box was full. I couldn't text him. He refused to use a smartphone.

I had to give up and go to work. When I reached my office, I closed the door and sat still for a long time. That was when I knew I was broken.

Because what had I almost done? What if I'd been able to find a parking spot?

No one in Pastoral Care knew anything about him. But of course they had noticed differences in me. The Head had knocked on my door.

"You feel like talking?"

I didn't. You can be someone broken, I was learning, and still get up and do your job.

I truly had not seen coming what came. Green Man was a fix-up, although I hadn't known that until after the fixing-up happened.

A cardiologist I'm friends with was leaving the medical center. I had often been invited to dinner with this woman and her wife. They never made me feel like a third wheel at their table; they were a couple who felt completely comfortable sitting around with someone single, so that it wasn't a couple plus one. We were just three people.

Now and then they'd give me advice. Become gay! You should be gay! I'd apologize.

When the cardiologist called me to come over for a good-bye dinner, because she and her wife were leaving for somewhere far away, I had no reason to think anyone else would be there.

And then the fix was on and that was that.

Green Man had dropped out of medical school so he could study, instead, plants that people a long time ago knew about for their healing properties. He became a medicinal botanist. He founded a lab he got funding for. The lab was in his building, in the apartment next to his own.

Everything about the two of us felt right to me. *We fit.* That was how I kept putting it. I began to feel at home with him pretty much the moment we met.

"Okay, who's the guy?"

My family was onto me early. Especially my sister. What did he play? What did he like to watch best? Basketball, or what? Did he go to a gym? Which one?

I said nothing.

Seven months. That was how long. We made love on his roof. We made love in his lab. The secrecy felt wonderful: a universe of two. I told him that my time with Plummy was practice for keeping something all my own.

We began to talk about the future. I was thinking about neighborhoods, about whether or not to take his name when we married. He wanted me to. It was a source of disagreement. And he didn't want us having parties and things where the guest list would contain ministers—it wouldn't be fair to mix his friends with people of mine from such a whole other world, like ministers don't know how to kick back and relax. Like it would be something like an alien invasion of wet blankets.

One member of the clergy was plenty enough for him. In myself, I was a whole universe of People of the Collar. I had liked the way he'd said that. He made me feel special. He made me feel that any other minister he'd come in contact with would have to be compared to me, and would only be a great disappointment.

I skipped the wedding of a good friend from seminary after declaring I'd be there, and I would not be coming alone. He had admitted he just wouldn't be able to cope with it. That weekend, he and I camped out on the roof and I fell more in love than ever.

I did not see the warning signs as actual warnings.

He didn't like coming to my development, where the blocks of units are laid out in rows off a main avenue, all the blocks the same, all tidy and well-maintained, and almost as sterile and business-like, he felt, as the medical center. He didn't like my apartment either; it made him feel boxed in and sort of trapped.

Sometimes I had the sense he was opening his life to me like it was a big new country for me to come live in, like he wanted me to emigrate from my own. But I would laugh at myself for being silly, for perhaps being someone it was hard to love.

One night, when I stayed late at the medical center, for almost a double shift, I came out of the building to find him in the parking lot, his car neatly, snugly blocking mine. I had called him many hours before to cancel our plans—I was supposed to go to his place as usual.

He followed me home. After everything I'd experienced in those hours at work, I loved coming out from my shower, still wet, to see him stretched out on my bed, the covers thrown off. He had spent the day in his lab. He smelled like plant life, like everything green and rooted, like his soul was green too.

I felt that my roots and his were inching toward each other a little more, were ready to be fully tangled up.

Then my phone beeped. Earlier that day, there was a terrible highway accident. The driver of a crowded bus had braked and swerved toward the breakdown lane to avoid colliding with the car of a driver who cut from the middle lane at the last minute, to make an exit. It was possible the car driver hadn't looked to see what was coming, and thought only of making his turn-off.

The bus struck that car, which had slowed, as there was a bottleneck of traffic on the exit ramp. The driver of the car behind the bus was not able to avoid crashing into it. There were four fatalities: the two car drivers, and two passengers in the second car.

Just before going off duty, I sat in a waiting room with the bus driver's family.

He was a longtimer who, it came out, had been in trouble before for highway speeding. No bus passengers required treatment, but he was badly injured, and had been taken into surgery. I left the medical center after hearing the news he was in a recovery room and his surgeon was optimistic about his chances.

I was being summoned back to his side. His family wanted no other chaplain, please, seeing as how I already knew them. He had gone through respiratory failure, and his heart was endangered; he had been placed in the ICU.

The vigil for his surgery gave way to a vigil of hope that his life would not end. He had not been able to communicate, but his family felt sure he was terrified he might be wrongly blamed for the accident. They wanted me to tell him to hang on and have faith, because God had not looked away from the road in the moments the crashes took place—that God would know none of it was his fault.

I had held his wife in my arms as she quivered and wept. I had bowed my head in prayer with the bus driver's sons, who were close to my own age. I had listened to stories of the man's life, as if telling the stories would be the one thing to make the surgery successful.

Green Man didn't want me to go. The medical center, he reminded me, didn't own me. There were night chaplains who could explain that I wasn't on duty. Surely the family would understand a chaplain's need for a private life.

He had already waited for me in the parking lot, as proof that he loved me, he pointed out. He was willing to put aside how much it made him unhappy to spend time in my home.

He patted the space on my bed where he wanted me to be. *Don't go.*

I thought that at the end of "Don't go" there was a "yet." I thought he might be saying I could postpone rushing back to the medical center, so we could first make love.

And I found myself counting minutes in my head, blocking out time: how long it would take me to get dry, get dressed, drive to the medical center. I was actually doing that arithmetic in my head. Really quick sex, I was thinking.

He meant it literally. *You can't go.*

How could he know me and not know that when I took off my collar, it was never really off?

It was strange to walk out of my own apartment when he was inside it. His voice was still loud in my ears as I stepped back out into the night.

The bus driver's last moments happened when I was next to him.

As his family had asked, I said to him, "God knows it wasn't your fault."

Three hours later, when I returned to my apartment, Green Man was gone. I had imagined he would wait for me.

He had taken back his keys. He had gone through my closet and drawers. He took a sweater of his I had borrowed one night, and a scarf I had borrowed too, and a pair of houseplants he had potted for me as a gift. And a dress he had bought me, exactly my size: dark-blue silk, luxurious, never worn.

The next day he did not return my calls.

The same was true the following day.

And the one after that.

And the one after that.

Everyone at work tiptoed around me, being weirdly polite. My parents kept calling me to come over for dinner. My sister sent texts saying things like, "You don't have to tell me what happened but I'm here for you." My brothers wanted to know, Who should we go beat up?

I called my friend the cardiologist, who didn't know anything, but contacted him after we spoke. All he would say was that he'd discovered the two of us were not compatible. She cried and apologized for misdiagnosing his basic character, in the first place.

The day before I drove to his building and couldn't park, I got home to find that he had mailed me a box of things I had left in his apartment: a toothbrush and my own brand of toothpaste, a pair of extra collars, a hooded sweatshirt, the blanket I'd bought special for going up to his roof. And also the gifts I had given him: a waterproof apron because he was always soaking himself when he watered plants, a rare book of botanical drawings, a bedside reading lamp because he hadn't had one for my side of his bed, and a polo shirt, because he'd suggested he should wear one when I brought him to meet my family, even though he hated polo shirts.

I saw him again only once, that following winter. I happened upon him in an open area for people waiting to bring home patients who came in for day surgery. He looked startled to see me, as if he'd forgotten where I work.

He was waiting for a guy who lived alone in his building, in for a minor procedure. He was being a good neighbor, but it was certainly taking a long time. He had already asked two different nurses what was happening, and they both said, no problems, we'll let you know when he's ready.

I asked him if he'd like me to check on that man.

He shook his head no, looking baffled. What was I talking about? They didn't let in visitors, or he would have gone himself.

"But I can go anywhere," I said.

I pointed to my collar, reminding him what it meant around here. I did so with a smile—yet I could see by his expression that I seemed to have made a wrong move.

He was on a cushioned bench with several other people. The waiting area was crowded. He was sitting at one end of the bench, looking up at me. He did not stand up. I'd been watching his face in the moment he heard me saying the words, "I can go anywhere."

He had never wanted me to be someone who goes anywhere. That was exactly what his face was saying to me.

And oh, by the way, he was planning a move. He'd been offered a big space for his lab. By whom, and where, he didn't say.

That evening, I went out to a bar with some nurses who were forever trying to get me out to a bar. They made me take off my collar. For the first time since I was in high school, I had too much to drink. I had to be driven home.

And what was it like to show up in Pastoral Care the next morning, bedraggled, wearing sunglasses because light hurt my eyes?

This was just a little while before we knew about the swing of the ax. The Head came over to me at the coffee maker. He didn't know anything, but he knew everything. He opened the drawer of the coffee table and took out a bottle of Advil, opened it, and handed me two.

The chaplain of the shortbread cookies had just walked in carrying a paper plate containing a huge cinnamon bun, still warm, glazed, multi-coiled. It was obvious he meant to take it to his own office, but after glancing at me, he put the plate in my hand. He apologized for his cookie tin being empty that day. He wanted to know if I'd like him to get me some scrambled eggs.

"You look so hungry," he had said.

I declined the eggs, but wolfed down the bun. They never asked, "Are you broken?" I will always remember how grateful I'd been, for that.

"Pizza!" called out a voice from my office doorway. "This the right place?"

Eighteen

I only had loose change for a tip.

The pizza guy was young and so skinny, he looked like he never in his life ate a carbohydrate. His mood was understandably edgy. He had delivered to the medical center tons of times before on the night shift, but finding my office wasn't easy—he'd had to go through a maze, and sure, tipping is officially optional, but *hey*.

The pizza was a large. He had set it down on my desk, which barely had room. The box was sticking out over the side. He took my coins, and did not seem interested in standing around while I searched my drawers, in case I had bills somewhere; Pastoral Care was always taking up collections for something.

I didn't find any more money, but I turned to go after him to tell him I'd stop by the pizza place soon. I wanted to ask his name. I wanted to see him again, and I didn't even realize it might have been for this reason: he reminded me a little of Plummy, six years ago.

As I stepped toward the hall, aware he'd made it away by now, I heard him in the distance, letting out an exclamation that sounded like a cry of surprise.

"Hey," I heard him saying. "Hey dude, what the hell?"

The dog came running into my office so fast, I had to flatten myself at the wall to not be knocked over. At the side of my desk, facing the pizza box, he skidded to a stop, with a bright fabric neck leash trailing behind him. Then he lowered himself to his haunches for a straight-back, head-high sit.

He was big. He was tan. He was a mix, but he was mostly a boxer.

The thrust of his muzzle announced that breed, along with his boxer jowls and the smooth, suede look of his coat, more like skin than fur. His age seemed neither young nor old. He was in his prime. Somewhere in his ancestry, there had to have been a mastiff, and possibly, by the slope of his forehead, and the way it was slightly furrowed, a pit bull as well. His ears were wide, oval flaps, velvety, of a deeper brown than the rest of him. His muzzle was the color of charcoal, and so were the markings that went upward past his nose, and underlaid his eyes. On his chest was a patch of white, like a bib. His paws were rimmed with white too, as if he wore socks. His tail was flecked with dark mini-streaks of brindle, like tattoos.

He was the fittest, most muscular, most athletic dog I'd ever been physically close to. It did not occur to me to be frightened of him—there was friendliness in the bright shine of his dark eyes, on top of his eagerness to be given human food. Already drool was dripping from him, looking like long, thin, melting icicles.

He was clean and well-groomed, and he must have been outdoors recently. He smelled lightly of the night and damp earth.

He didn't look at me, coming to him, taking small steps, my hand extended.

He took himself seriously, I saw. And he had certainly received an education. Right away, I started thinking of him as Mrs. Copp's dog, but I knew he belonged to the people of Bobo Boy. I recognized the leash with its tie-dyed colors, and the matching collar, tags dangling. Perhaps, like Bobo Boy, he refused to wear the vest that's supposed to be the uniform of a therapy dog. He might have shredded one, or maybe several. His teeth were enormous.

He must have gotten away from his handler. I realized I was expecting his human to make an appearance, perhaps out of breath from chasing him. But there was no one.

Dignity. He was an animal of dignity, sitting like that.

"Hi," I said. "I have to tell you, you're pretty amazing, but I bet you know that about yourself. If I were you, I'd have grabbed that box. Gooey cheese would be hanging from my lips, not drool."

I had eaten pizza before from the all-night place, with various nurses and doctors. They made it so greasy, I'd dab at the top with a paper napkin before digging in, but I didn't bother about that now, because why make the dog wait while I went to find some napkins?

The biggest tag attached to his collar was silver, in the shape of a heart. His name was etched there. Eddie.

I touched my hand to the top of his head, briefly, palm flat. Then I opened the box, saying, "Eddie. You're Eddie."

His ears flicked in recognition, but he was otherwise completely motionless.

"I heard about you," I said. "And someone told me you're not supposed to be real."

I loosened a slice and tore off the crust. He didn't lunge for it. He took it almost delicately. I thought he'd lie down and chew on it like a bone, but he devoured it in a matter of seconds.

I worked our way through half the pizza, giving him, each time, a portion of slices too. He looked sad when I closed the box.

"Sorry, but we're not going to overdo it," I told him.

The box didn't fit into the little Pastoral Care fridge, so I placed the remaining slices inside on their wax paper lining. While I tore up the cardboard for the wastebasket, he stared at me as if he wanted to eat that too.

Got goop?

I . . . feel I am a . . . car . . . toooon.

The voice of Mrs. Copp was playing itself back to me, coming from deep inside me, rising up clearly, exactly as the old woman had sounded in life. Seizing a paper towel from the coffee area, and wiping my hands, I felt all over again what it was like to grasp hold of those dentures. To have the teeth of someone in my palm. To look at the toothless mouth, so weirdly beautiful in its pinkness, tenderness, weakness, babylike frailness, birdlike strength.

It does not make sense to say I felt I held a part of the soul of that person in my hand. That it was doing something to my own—not that I could understand what the something was.

But of course what I really had held was a set of false teeth.

"This is kind of an unusual night, Eddie," I said.

Tomato sauce was on his chin. He had licked around his muzzle with his enormous tongue, but missed that spot. He let me dab at him with the paper towel.

I had just been paged again—what to do? I supposed I could keep him with me like I'd been newly recruited as a handler. And so, confidently, I picked up his leash and slipped my hand in the loop, trusting that his excellent manners would continue.

But the silent, dignified dog had other ideas. He bolted forward, yanking me so hard, I nearly lost my balance. I didn't dare let go of the leash. He was my responsibility, at least for now.

He ignored me when I told him to stop. Some training!

But I hung on, thankful he eased up his pace enough for me to proceed at a brisk walk. His head was lowered, nose way down, like we were out in the woods out back and he was tracking. He did not glance back to see how I was doing. What I thought of him and his behavior, he didn't care.

We passed a small group of aides talking together, pausing to laugh at the sight of the chaplain being tugged along.

A housekeeper pushing a cart of supplies called out, "Reverend, who's walking who here?"

We turned a corner, another. I could hear him panting, ahead of me. The leash was taut, at its fullest. The loop was digging into my hand.

Then he stopped and turned into a consultation room, which I had often used on the day shift to speak with families and friends of patients in some sort of danger, as well as loved ones of someone who just moments ago had passed, and they couldn't bear the thought of leaving the hospital. The Consolation Room, it's called, and there, in one of the plush armchairs, was a young woman who used to be a handler of Bobo Boy.

I hadn't seen this woman for quite a while. She wore the long, loose, green vest of the agency, the sides pushed back. Her jersey was striped brightly: red, yellow, blue, orange, like a beach ball.

She looked about six or seven months pregnant, possibly more. She was asleep.

I let go of the leash. Eddie finally turned his head to acknowledge me. His tongue was hanging straight down from the center of his mouth, and he flapped it a bit, while his tail moved sideways in a wag.

He looked proud of himself, lowering himself to the floor by the armchair, settling down.

"Well there he is, the devil," whispered a voice behind me.

It was Guy RN, towering above me, his scrubs quite rumpled and soiled. He had a mass of hair as white and fluffy as the silk of a milkweed. His eyeglasses were low on his nose, and he was peering down at me, his eyes showing their usual friendly, kind shine.

He was the first male nurse the medical center hired, years before I arrived. His name tag actually said "Guy RN." The human resources people gave up a long time ago trying to make him wear a normal one.

He had recently remarried, after a divorce I knew he'd taken hard. Briefly, when he had wanted to start dating, he went around with a homemade, larger badge that said, "Fight stereotypes! Women! Ask me if I'm straight!" He'd gotten in trouble for that.

I hadn't seen him before on the night shift. He'd been called in to help out with all the injuries.

"Could've been worse," he told me, keeping his voice low. "And this dog here, unbelievable. They shouldn't have brought him in. And just look at him, all innocence. I get it that they'd come to help, comfort-animal like, but they should've waited till things were less crazy."

"What happened?"

"Let's just say Mr. Boxer there thinks no one should give him orders but himself. This poor woman—she has to wait for someone to pick them up. I don't think she expected to be thrown out of the ER. Did you know they get their dogs as rescues out of pounds?"

"I knew that."

"This one," he said, pointing at Eddie, "was a stray. Lucky for him, someone picked him up before Animal Control did. The agency doesn't have a clue where he'd been before."

"I think he has a really high IQ," I said. "I mean, I'm guessing, just looking at him."

Eddie had turned his head away. I had the feeling he knew we were discussing him, and he decided it was beneath him to react.

"He's not beyond redemption, Reverend. We had a store employee freaking out because he couldn't find his girlfriend. He thought she was still under the rubble, but it turned out, she's in another hospital. Mr. Boxer went up to him. You know how, when they're going to do their business, they circle around the spot they're about to do it on? He did that. Went around and around maybe four times. This man, he had to stop the freak-out, just out of curiosity. Soon as he calmed down, Mr. Boxer was jumping him, hands right up against his chest. I mean, sorry, paws right up against his chest. Slobbered all over him, and the man, what else could he do? He started laughing his head off. He was all, 'I don't even like dogs.' It's not your usual comfort thing, but it sure did work. How are you doing, by the way?"

I remembered my page. "I think I'll be glad when this night is over," I said. "I've got to run."

Guy RN pulled the door of the Consolation Room closed.

"Let's allow the mama-to-be her sleep," he said. "And I know Mr. Boxer will stay put in here."

I wanted to tell him about my feeling he might be wrong about that—I didn't want to seem irrational. I hurried toward an elevator. I looked out a window I passed, for any sign of gray morning dusk, gathering like clouds of smoke. But it was all just dark, just still completely all night.

Nineteen

"Did you ever see pictures of angels, in books, or in churches or museums?"

A few nights ago, the teller asked this question of the aide who was changing her bedclothes. The aide had nodded yes; everyone knows what angels look like.

"Do you know why angels have arms in all the pictures?"

"I'll go find your chaplain," the aide had answered.

But that night, when I reached her side, the teller hadn't spoken of angels. It was only the usual greeting, the usual sitting.

Her aloneness was all around her like an extra layer of air. She had been ill so long, it was hard to get a sense of who she was before she was sick. Or where she was inside herself, beneath the rough and brittle shell her illness had turned her body into.

She was supposed to be transferred to a hospice place, but it was decided she was too fragile. I knew there were issues about insurance, about who would pay for what. The medical center is not a charity!

I knew what it felt like to hear that kind of thing. Yet somehow people like the teller fell sometimes into the right sort of crack. For her, the crack was right here.

She was being kept as comfortable as possible. She was now in a zone of the dusky space between staying and leaving, the waiting area of passing.

"I'm here," I said, bending toward her, laying a hand on her arm.

For the first time, there was no response. She wasn't lying there saying, "Hi. I'm your teller."

She was in late middle age but looked elderly. Soon after she finished high school, she went to work in a local savings bank as a trainee at the counter, and for almost forty years she remained there, sometimes running the drive-up window, sometimes filling in for a front receptionist on vacation. The bank was folded into a national one early in her employment. She had spoken to a nurse, in a rare conversation, of her old fear she'd lose her job in the take-over, as if there were no other banks she could go to, no other job she could consider.

It was known that she'd been married, but it had ended in divorce. Her next of kin was listed as a brother, who for some reason was unable to come see her. Day shifters had noted in her file that she hadn't once had a visitor.

Her religious affiliation was given as "I left my church for personal reasons." But she had indicated she would welcome visits from a chaplain.

Her nights had been restless, as she was no longer aware of day and night. She was admitted to the medical center after someone who worked in the management of her apartment building went to see her, for not having paid her rent.

It turned out that she was treated previously at another hospital, where they released her in the belief she'd enter hospice care at home. But no arrangements were ever made for that—no visiting nurses, no supervision of medications, no aide, no anything. An ambulance had been called, and here she was.

The teller was never interested in talking with me, not even at those times, at four or five in the morning, she was fully a stranger to sleep. So I had tried a different approach.

I created a delusion for us. I told this woman that the bank where she worked was my own. Actually, I belong to a credit union.

"You used to be my teller," I had said. "It's okay you don't remember me. I can't imagine how many customers you faced all those years. But I certainly remember you."

After that, I would enter the room and receive a smile.

"Hi. I'm your teller. It's nice to see you again."

We had looked at each other in a silence that never felt wrong or awkward. Maybe it was all those years in the bank, side by side with her workmates, speaking always quietly, only sharing bits of small talk in a lull, or saying nothing at all.

Or it was all those years of going home to a place where if you spoke out loud, no one was there to hear you.

"Bye from your teller," she used to say, when a visit from her chaplain had come to an end.

And now she was entering her last moments. I was in the chair beside her. A nurse had just come in, checking her. Not long now. I nodded, knowing.

As the minutes ticked by, I was busy trying to think of what to say. Should I ask if she wanted prayers? Would the teller want to speak of her soul? Of her life, of what had meaning to her, of what was holy to her?

Then all of a sudden, she wanted to talk.

Lying there, she was bone-thin. She weighed barely more than a child. But not in her own mind.

Her voice was strangely clear, although its tone was a little muffled. She was obviously anxious, worried.

She was telling me that the angel who just entered the room was all wrong, and please, being her chaplain, would I do something about that? It seemed that the angel had been refusing to do what the teller wanted: go away and send in the right one.

The problem, I learned, was a problem with size. It was too little.

I also learned that the angel was neither male nor female, not particularly, not so you could tell. It was very, very slender. And would I take note of its height? How could an angel be so short?

Basically, a great mistake had been made. This angel was unsuitable for the job of carrying the teller off the earth, and then across all the distance to God.

To make things worse, it was standing there scowling and looking angry, as if the teller were busy in her bed with thinking up new ways to insult it. Obviously, the angel had no experience being criticized, never mind rejected.

And would I look at those arms? Those arms were *scrawny*.

The teller was afraid of being dropped. She didn't want an angel who might not even have the strength to lift her out of bed.

I listened to her. Her voice was growing whispery and hoarse and raspy. Long pauses took place between many of her words. But she was getting her words out. She could have been back at work, talking about a customer who wanted her to cash a check against an account that did not have the right amount of money, and the customer was refusing to believe her. I could have been a supervisor called over to handle the fuss.

Hesitating, trying to make up my mind which course of action to take, I bowed my head. The teller was watching me carefully, trusting me. Should I talk to the angel from my chair? Should I stand and approach it, speaking directly into its ear, in whispers, privately?

There were three other beds in this room, all occupied. Nurses and aides came and went. The teller's roommates were newly post-surgical and required much attention.

The curtains around her bed had been partially drawn, so that she was shielded for privacy from the beds opposite and beside hers. There was not much room between the foot of the bed and the curtain the angel was inside of. If I went over to the foot, I would need to figure out a way to position myself. I would need to stand in a space that was not already taken.

I could not allow it to happen that I bumped into the angel—or worse, accidentally knocked it over.

And what tone of voice should I use, even in whispers? Should I be forceful, bossy? Should I be kind and respectful, so the teller wouldn't worry I'd ruffle feathers that weren't already ruffled?

Or, should I explain to her that the size and strength of her angel were just right, because her body was so small now, so light?

I felt a tightening of the fingers of the hand I was holding. The teller was raising her head, about an inch or so off her pillow. Her eyes were looking toward the foot of the bed. She was blinking very rapidly. I saw that those eyes were filling with tears.

And I knew they weren't tears because of anything being wrong. When the teller spoke again, she didn't mention size or strong arms. She had forgotten all about me, but she seemed to feel that her chaplain had come through for her. The little angel had just grown tremendously, and suddenly developed some muscles—or it had disappeared, and the one in its place was a giant, perhaps with a head almost touching the ceiling.

"It's so bright," said the teller, mumbly, softly, in a tone of voice that was very matter of fact.

But when she repeated it, as her last thing to say, it came in the voice of someone being taken by surprise, like she could not believe her own eyes.

"It's so *bright*!"

I sat there. I listened to the new sound of silence. I looked at the nurse who was noting the time of the departure. I didn't know how much the nurse heard of what the teller had said, but she was glancing around, almost as if she hoped to hear some sound in the air that had not been there before.

I went out to the hall. I thought I'd go sit in another waiting room for a few minutes. But the one on this hall was being cleaned.

Then all I could think of was that I needed more coffee. I was being practical. I remembered that on the floor below, there was often good coffee in the unit kitchen. The teller's room was near an exit.

Maybe I've always been a little clumsy in the aftermath of a passing, and I was only just now noticing. I realized too late I should have gone for an elevator. On the stairway, I overshot the top step, and I went into a panic, feeling myself slipping, feeling myself falling.

I didn't see Eddie until he reached the landing I was about to crash on. He was walking up the stairs—I heard the light thumps of his paws, the little jangle of his tags.

The stairwell filled with the smell of dog. His big boxer eyes were shiny. His head was high, his ears perked up. He was coming toward me, his leash trailing behind him. He was not in a rush, not in a state of alarm.

He was calm, and why did it feel like I was falling the wrong way now? Why was I going up, not down?

How could I suddenly be falling *up*?

"Hang on," the dog seemed to be telling me, with a look.

I grabbed the leash. The ceiling was collapsing—but no, wait, it wasn't like what happened at the scene of the disaster. The roof was opening. There might have been a panel there all along, like a sunroof on a car, somehow being activated.

The loop of the leash was now around my hand. I was climbing stairs of air, toward the opening, Eddie at my heels. Then I realized I didn't have to actually climb.

I was just rising, just floating, just rising and floating and rising, and it all seemed perfectly normal, perfectly natural, like I was anyone at all who ever went out into the last dark hour of a night, taking a dog for a walk.

Twenty

Eddie pawed at the air, as if swimming, but he seemed to be doing so in play, knowing that air isn't water.

We were headed for the highway, at a rate of speed neither fast nor slow. I realized I did not have a say in what direction to take, any more than a feather on a breeze would, but why should that matter when you're up in the air?

Bobo Boy's linden! We sailed over it, the top of its crown right under my feet. Looking back, I saw a pair of nurses smoking cigarettes outside the entrance to the ER, near the sign that said "No Smoking." One of them was glancing up, and I waved, and that was how I knew we were invisible.

There were very few vehicles on the highway. A milk delivery truck rolled by; a young man was one-handing the wheel. He was about to sip from a Dunkin' Donuts cup of coffee. I could tell the coffee was too hot. His lips were puckered. I was looking at him in the act of blowing into the sip hole of the lid, and I felt worried for him, hoping he wouldn't burn his tongue.

In a small Ford sedan, a woman about my age, alone, reached up to adjust her rearview mirror. She was checking her appearance. She had just put on lipstick. Why would she have done that, risking it, one hand on the wheel? Yet wearing fresh lipstick was important to her. Why was she traveling at this hour?

"I hope things go well for you," I was trying to say, as if being a chaplain to drivers was my job now.

The amazing thing was that I did not feel amazed.

Grace, I thought, because I realized I had never known before what the word really means.

It means that suddenly there comes a moment when you are all right.

Nothing is wrong.

The simplicity felt as beautiful to me as the air around me, as my lightness, as I was air too, and so was Eddie, his head high, his tail swishing: grace in the form of a dog.

I looked down again. In the passenger's seat of a Volvo sedan, a girl of about eleven was typing with her thumbs on her iPhone, huddled up with it, the glow a rectangular patch of light that looked odd to me, even though I owned the same phone. I couldn't see the words the girl was texting. I couldn't see who was driving, except that the person was a grown-up.

The girl had turned in her seat so that her back was to the driver. I had a feeling of her loneliness, a feeling that her text was like the words of a sad, deep-reaching song. Then I saw a pause in the typing. The girl was tipping back her head, peering out her window, looking upward, as if noticing a ray of moonlight or an unusually low cloud.

Her expression seemed to brighten—perhaps, for an instant, because of me and Eddie, she was not quite so all alone? It was impossible to tell.

Coming behind the Volvo was a small blue Ford. On its back seat, a white terrier was curled up, its eyes drowsily half-lidded. Spotting the dog before I did, Eddie let out call-barks, in a greeting, in a happy, friendly tone. I felt proud of him. He was a charmer! He was sociable to other dogs!

But loud as Eddie was, the terrier did not respond to him, not even to perk up its ears a little bit. It was the same as if no sounds had been made. I couldn't tell if it bothered Eddie that he was invisible to everyone but me, and he couldn't make contact with a member of his species, fleeting as it would have been.

He had moved out in front of me. He was letting me know he wanted me to follow him, as if he'd picked up a new scent. It seemed he was zeroing in on a set of directions, like he was tuned into a special GPS, for just dogs.

He quickened his pace, pulling me along, the same way he did before, post-pizza. There was no way for me to know how far we'd gone, or how long we'd been moving.

I was not aware of the moment when this happened, but we were not on the highway anymore. We were floating along a countryside road, full of curves. We were passing rows and rows of high, wide trees, fallow fields, stone walls of old farms, ancient looking graveyards, iron fences the color of creosote and so much darker than the night. I saw a barn in a state of collapsing and a development of brand new Colonials: mini-mansions set back from the road at the end of long driveways, where globes of solar lights had been poked into the ground, and could almost seem like gatherings of fireflies.

Once, I remembered, on a summer night when I was small and weak from some flu that was going around, my brothers came into my room and woke me. I always seemed to be hit the hardest by viruses that were minor to everyone else. That one had lasted quite awhile, and suddenly there they were, the two of them, my big brothers, ready to amaze me.

They used to drive me crazy when they'd tap their knuckles against my forehead, as if knocking on a door. They'd feel weird and uncomfortable whenever they came upon me sitting still, head bowed, or lying outside in the yard, my eyes on the sky, like I was an athlete of things that only took place inside you. I had baffled them, baffled them all.

"Earth to Little Pinkie," they would say, knocking at me. "Anyone home in there?"

But that night, they were not making fun of me.

"Earth to Little Pinkie! We filled the backyard with fairies for you!"

I had believed my brothers arranged a sort of concert for me, but it was a concert of lights, not sound. I hadn't known that the creatures outside my window were insects called fireflies.

But I never told them I didn't believe they were fairies. In my joy, I felt they were tiny pieces of souls of happy people, blinking on and off, gloriously, thrilling me: souls that belonged somewhere else, but came out into the night to make me feel better.

I wished I could pause and tell all of that to Eddie, as if maybe, in this state, an animal and a person could actually have a conversation. I realized, though, I did not have the power to stop moving.

We had reached a section of the road where a gap was showing in a broad, thick wall of trees. Because of the way the treetops on either side seemed to bend toward each other, arch-like, the gap looked like an open entryway.

Eddie was making a turn toward the opening. There was a destination? Which he knew about, and I didn't?

He seemed to sense my hesitation. He turned his head to look at me with his bright boxer eyes. He was showing me the tawny sheen of his fur, his smoothness, his strong chest, his muzzle, his snout, darker and blacker than the night. He was showing me his soul, in every part of himself, and he seemed to be asking, Would I please just follow his lead? Would I please just really trust him?

Twenty-one

There was a drop in my elevation. I drifted into the turn, through the gap in the trees, and found myself in a small country lane bordered by tall old maples, their branches filled with cobwebs of fog, rustling a little on a light and skittery wind. The air smelled watery. I knew for sure I'd never been here before.

A building was up ahead. As slowly as I was moving, I was getting nervous—I had no power to stop. I could only move forward.

And I realized I was alone. That dog had abandoned me?

Well probably it was my own fault. We barely knew each other!

I called to him, once, twice, three times. I didn't want to give up trying, but my shouts were being folded into the hush of the night, the same as if they'd never been made.

The building I approached was low and solitary, with barn-board walls of pine. Its shape was like that of a train car or a trailer, sitting sideways, but that was just the front section. On either side was an added-on wing, so that the wholeness was like the letter "E," tipped flat, without the middle line. To my left was a door above a small wooden stoop. Some sort of plaque was hanging there, but I couldn't make it out.

The two squares of windows were curtained. Lights were on inside, dimly. I thought I detected some movement inside, like slow-motion flickers of shadows.

The curtains were thin and gauzy. It would have been easy to see through them, if not for their printed patterns. At first, the bright, colorful shapes that covered the cloth reminded me of the Teletubbies, plump and happy in their cartoon selves, waddling around in the colors of candy, or popsicles: lime, lemon, cherry, grape purple.

Teletubbies! Rolling down hills, skipping through meadows! Chattering to each other in secret baby talk about how splendid everything was, how they were splendid too! How many hours had I spent watching those videos with tiny patients? Many, many hours.

But the figures on the curtains weren't Teletubbies. They only resembled them, in the same colors, rolling in grass, smelling a flower, bumping into each other. They were cartoons of dogs, all sorts of dogs—puppies, young dogs, old dogs, all sorts of breeds and mixes. Some were so whimsical, they did not exist for real, like the creatures of the banished poster.

And then I was inside the building, and it was a huge disappointment not to know how I got there.

My brothers used to tease me for being a little girl playing their *Star Trek* videos while clutching the remote so I could fast-forward to the transporter scenes. I had loved those scenes. I had hoped that someone would invent a transporter for real by the time I became a grown-up.

I never had anywhere in particular I wanted to go—I just wanted to understand how it would feel to be a pulsing, glittering, shimmering, body-shaped mass of energy and dots of light, as if what happened in a transport was that your body and soul switched places, in a marvelous, inside-out way.

I had told this to Plummy. He had felt the need to pop my bubble by rattling off every time someone dies in a transporter accident, in all the various *Star Trek*s.

It was only a minor conversation—one I didn't expect him to refer to again. But soon after he'd arrived in Germany, he emailed to say, if I would agree to come visit him regularly, he would get in touch with a genius engineer he went to college with, who owed him a favor. He would get the engineer to build us transporters, one hundred percent safe. Thus we could both be where we were and carry on as a couple, just take up where we'd left off, like we were supposed to.

And how had he decided on what we were supposed to do?"

"Logic," he had told me, like he was Spock. "Me and you together make a solution to a problem that can't be solved any other way."

And what was the problem?

"We're both lonely people no one else would ever want to put up with, not with how we both are, basically."

I was not a lonely person! People could put up with me!

I would never be able to keep track of all the times I wished I had sent him away that day in the chapel on my birthday when he wanted to know if I knew of any oobs and why I looked so sad.

I had even glossed over the fact he had said he loved to call oobs oobs because it's "boobs" without the first "b."

To a minister in a collar he'd just met, he had said this. Like he was twelve! And I had almost laughed because he said it so seriously.

I hadn't been sad! I was not a sad person!

"This is pretty cool," he would have whispered, if he were beside me.

I was in a reception area. Night-lights were on, in shapes of little candles, plugged into several wall sockets. There was a counter, wooden and smooth and old, as one might find in a municipal office, or a bank or a courthouse. Beyond the counter were some desks, computers, all the usual office-type stuff.

A wall rack stuffed with brochures was near a small round table with a couple of chairs. A plastic clock with a face of Hello Kitty was ticking away, and it was dangling a plastic tail of a cat, back and forth, back and forth, back and forth. A large poster showed a trio of dogs sitting closely together on the steps of some-one's backyard deck: an elderly and jowly bulldog, a young brindle greyhound, and a brown-and-white Chihuahua puppy. At the top were the words "THESE 3 SISTERS BELIEVE." At the bottom was the rest of the message: "IN ADOPTION."

I noticed titles of brochures as I floated by the rack: *A Guide to Do-It-Yourself Grooming; Worm Treatment Explained; Five Reasons Why Your Dog Might Be Chewing Your Shoes.*

On the floor were linoleum tiles, worn, many-times mopped. How many feet had trod here, how many paws, how many accidental peeings and poopings?

Shabbiness, I saw. And decency.

A decency of shabbiness. That was my overall impression, especially around the area of the desks, where everything looked like it came secondhand, and would soon need replacing. But I had the feeling that the people who sat at those desks were people who would know what I was talking about if I came here in the normal way and suddenly started talking about souls and how empty it can be if you understand the fact that the one you have has been broken.

From a pair of printed statements in frames on another wall, I learned that this was a privately run place for dogs and cats who were saved by volunteers from *high-kill establishments.* They had twenty-four-hour staffing, but potential adopters were restricted to normal work hours. They did not encourage people who wished to surrender a pet to use their shelter, since they were non-public and always stretched to their maximum with animals transported here, often from great distances.

"We believe," I read, "that animals are no lesser creatures than we are. We are small and we struggle financially. We ask all visitors, whether or not you go home with one of our residents, to please make a contribution, in whatever amount is okay for you. Thanks!"

Why did I have to be invisible? Why couldn't I reach for my wallet?

Meanwhile, on top of the counter, two large calico cats were sprawled out, one fat and one lean. They were facing away from each other, their tails touching at the tips and overlapping a little, like that was their way of feeling connected. They seemed to have no idea I was looking at them. Their breathing stayed the same: the breathing of sleepers. I began to drift closer to them, eager to see what they might do if they sensed me.

They did not react. Not one whisker even twitched a tiny bit. Maybe they were being aloof, on purpose. Maybe they were letting me know it was no big deal to them to see me, like they were saying, "We look at invisible things all the time, and frankly, we don't think you're interesting."

But then I was moving again, more urgently, into a wing of the building, a sort of wide hallway. On either side were cells.

No, not cells. This was not a prison. They were cubicles. Or they were cages, but not actually cages. They were tiled inside like shower stalls and fronted by wooden frames holding panels of Plexiglas.

Inside the not-cells, all the dogs were sleepers. A few were doubled, as if they'd fallen asleep in each other's arms, but most were alone. Some were on cushions of dog beds, some on cots, like something a camper might use, but smaller. Some were curled nearly in circles, noses close to tails. Some were stretched out on their sides, back legs overshooting a cot or cushion, like someone too tall for their own mattress. A few were in a huddle of their own selves in a corner, the cushion or cot unused.

I heard no snoring, no utterances from the depths of some dream, but that might have been happening because my ears had stopped being able to take in sound. I was fully muffled, I realized, in a cocoon of a hush that was just like the hush of the chapel.

You can't enter the dreams of someone else to say hi and wish them well and *It's dark but we have to believe there will be light, and we will be right about that.* If I thought I could knock on the doors of people's dreamlands, I'd be going around the medical center every night with my hand raised for the act of knocking.

But this wasn't just any night and I wasn't at the medical center and these sleepers were not people.

My prayer for them came to me like words of a song I'd already known the melody of. I was telling them all that I hoped they did not have the sense, in their not-cages, they would be there for the rest of their lives. I was telling them about the librarian and her clot and how afraid she was and how I'd be seeing her again soon. I was telling them about the lawyer and his cloud and his joy. I was telling them about a forever-broken-body boy who was young enough to not be broken in his soul, or maybe it was because, lonely as he was, he was born to luck out with the power of an ocean. I was telling them about Mrs. Copp and how I believed that what was holy to her was her own self.

I was telling them what I had not been able to tell the librarian in my awful silence before I lucked out myself and saw she had talked her way into sleeping: whatever they'd been through already, whatever they felt in their darkest moments, *Please imagine what hope is, and please then have it.*

And may you all in the morning go outdoors in sunlight and roll around like Teletubbies, I was praying, as I was moving along, a little faster, to the other wing.

The wing of the cats!

I passed a large room with walls largely made of window glass. I saw cages, cat shapes, cat fur, orange, gray, striped, black, white, not all sleeping: shiny eyes, looking my way, perhaps sensing me? But I wasn't going into that room, although I would have liked to.

I was headed for . . . a parlor?

That's what it looked like: an old-fashioned parlor with furniture that might have come from someone's grandparents, or an estate auction or yard sale where, at the end, they give away stuff for free, just to be rid of it. The door was open. A card on the wall said, "Meet and Greet Room."

I saw a darkly upholstered, saggy, frayed-edges sofa and a pair of old armchairs with vinyl coverings that looked almost like leather. The walls were softly yellow. There were no lamps, just a ceiling light of a bulb in a dome, low-wattage, giving off a gentle sheen of light. The pictures in frames on the walls were photographs of people with pets: dogs on leashes heading out of the building, cats in carry-crates or in someone's arms.

I entered. On the couch, a woman was sleeping, in a seated position, her head neither tipped back nor bowed. It looked like she hadn't meant to doze off.

The rug on the floor was a braided one, oval, the fibers so worn, the braidings were smoothed out and flattened. A dog was lying on this rug, on her side, eyes closed, a pillow under her head: a bed pillow, no doubt brought here from someone's home. The pillowcase was flowery, all pink and light green.

She was a dog in the category of Large: black and brown, a mix, partly German Shepherd, partly mastiff, partly a little boxer too. Her body was thin. She wasn't so thin that her ribs were showing, but her ribs were showing almost. Her muzzle had the gray of old age. It appeared her health had been poor for quite some time. But she did not seem in pain.

On one of the vinyl armchairs was a sheet of paper. The lettering was in thick black marker.

> THERE IS NOWHERE ELSE TO LEAVE THIS DOG.
> SHE IS NOT OKAY.
> IT IS ALL TOO MUCH TO HANDLE.
> PLEASE DON'T THINK WE'RE BAD PEOPLE.
> THANK YOU.

Her breathing was slow, almost languid. A bowl of water was on the floor. A small square of terrycloth was in the bowl too. The sleeping woman, I realized, was a shelter staffer, keeping a vigil, giving water to the dog by squeezing the cloth.

And finally I was ready to look at the other armchair, at the dog sitting there, his whole self wide awake. He was meeting my eyes as if asking the question, What took you so long to find me?

"Hi, Eddie," I said.

I was bursting with questions. Had he ever lived in this place? The agency had taken him in as a stray, I remembered. Was he adopted from here? Had he fled whoever adopted him, and if so, why? I was sure he'd never do anything without a good reason. Did he know this dog?

All I could do was hope he understood I knew he'd brought me here to be a chaplain at a passing.

I was able to descend to the floor, to hover by the animal whose name I didn't know. It was the same as if I'd entered the ER to be with someone brought in with no identification.

I glanced again at the woman on the couch, and saw the face of someone overcome by exhaustion. I imagined the touch of that woman's hands on animal fur, the sound of her voice, soothing a frightened dog, a confused dog, a lonely one. Maybe she was a night-shift regular. Maybe she had worked all day and her shift had been extended, and someone had left their sick old dog here, perhaps outside the front door. Perhaps she had strained herself, carrying the dog indoors. Perhaps the pillow was her own, for naps on that couch.

The woman seemed another version of Eddie's pregnant handler, not that she was pregnant in a beach ball jersey. She was a little overweight, her body shaped like a pear. On her feet were bright-purple Crocs. She wore denim overalls, baggy, far from new. A folded bandana served as a headband. Her hair reminded me of my own—but on her it was an Afro. She was lightly brown, and freckled, the tiny darker circles dotting her face below her eyes.

The bandana had slipped down a bit, on the way to becoming a blindfold. I wished I had the power to go over to her and gently, gently push it back in place.

Eddie left the armchair and settled down beside me. His breath was going in and out in the rhythms of the dog on the floor, and so was mine, as if he and I were a little sedated.

Then I saw that the eyelids of the dog on the floor were lifting, so that her eyes were neither all the way open nor all the way closed.

"You're full of grace, and I see that, you beautiful animal," I told her.

That's what I used to say all the time to Bobo Boy. Eddie just watched, just observing, like a medical student. I was under no delusion either of us could break through to her, but suddenly I knew she was aware of us. Here, now, it didn't matter what could be seen or unseen in the way of physical eyes.

I watched that dog gather up whatever force she still had—her whole self became focused on sending a signal. She was willing herself to speak, somehow. And just when I thought the effort would fail, she managed some movements: a slight little rise of her tail, up and down a few times, with the sounds of soft, mild thumping.

I heard those sounds, when all along in my hush, I couldn't hear anything else. I heard the thumps on the braided rug, like a talking tail in action.

The dog was saying a hello to us, like a patient in a bed, glad and surprised to have visitors.

Maybe this was just me, reading something into the dog that really wasn't happening, but I felt that she was thinking of the sleeping woman, of her kindness, her touch. She wanted to hang on. I felt that, if she were close to the place of last moments, she was hoping she wouldn't do her passing in the moments before the woman woke. She didn't want the woman to open her eyes and her ears to the new stillness.

I think Eddie's presence gave her strength. I think he knew that, like that was his job.

I felt myself turning. The two calico cats had just appeared in the parlor doorway, silently, one stout and one lean, watching. It seemed to me they knew exactly what they were doing, and why they had felt they needed to make the journey from the front counter: to help out with the vigil.

"You did great. I think it's time for us to go, Eddie," I said.

He looked like he agreed with me that we needed to return to the feel of our own heartbeats, like beats of a background percussion, tapping and tapping, like the dog on the floor, moving her tail again, in just very small sounds. But it seemed a whole band was playing music, and all the instruments were drums.

Twenty-two

It's so bright!

The light on the ceiling burned whitely into my eyes, not that I knew at this moment where I was, or how I came to be here.

A woman in Housekeeping had just found me in the stairwell. She did not seem alarmed that the night chaplain was blinking her eyes in a daze, and appeared to be stuck. I was lying on the steps at a very odd angle, as if I'd tried to coast down on an invisible sled, and managed only to run into the railing.

The housekeeper showed no surprise when the first thing I did was ask a question she could not have expected.

"Where's that dog?"

She had only just arrived. She was sorry, but she hadn't seen one. And that was a pity to her, because unlike most housekeepers, she was fond of having them around, in spite of the extra required cleanup. You always have to be on the lookout for shed fur, so awful in terms of being sanitary in a hospital—but it's not like the therapy animals go around dropping pieces of their coats on purpose.

She had witnessed the effects they have on patients. Bringers of smiles, they are. She had lived by herself since her divorce a few years ago, and her children were grown and had flown the nest, so she took the plunge into having a companion: a brown-and-black Chihuahua she adopted from a shelter. She had thought about having him trained for therapy work, but he does not have a positive outlook about anything outside their home. He enjoys most of all to run around yapping and expressing his opinions; he thinks humans are stupid and dangerous, except for her.

But there might have been a dog a little while ago on these stairs, seeing as how the reverend has said so. She sniffed the air. She couldn't say for sure that she wasn't picking up a little bit of an odor. They do leave smells behind.

It seemed the reverend had not been injured. And thank God for that!

She was coming into the hall from cleaning the waiting room when she heard a strange thump. She thought that someone carrying a heavy object had dropped it. She had decided to investigate only because she worried she might have imagined it. Some nurses were right nearby, and did not detect a thing.

"And look, the box no one dropped is you, Reverend," she was saying.

I felt I was being ministered to. I was shaken, light-headed, dizzy, and afraid to stand up. She realized I had fainted, had lost consciousness. And here was this person, talking and talking and talking, wrapping me in a cocoon of words, in the melodies of a soft, friendly voice.

I saw a wide, smiling face, so pale white it seemed to me for a moment the woman might actually be a patient. A pale-blue hair scarf covered her head, tied in the back, fitting her snugly, as if she'd lost her hair due to chemo—but that was wrong. She wore the loose, tunic-type top of the housekeepers, the same color as the scarf.

Everything about her expression was saying, "I will help you, not judge you."

"Reverend," she said, "should you go and let a doctor or a nurse have a look at you? I can tell you're not hurt, but what if possibly you hit your head? A neighbor of mine took a fall in her yard not long ago and thought nothing of it, as she landed on grass. But it was a nasty thing afterward and she was found to have a concussion. I only say so out of concern. You and I have not crossed paths before but I know you're well regarded. I don't think Our Lord would want you to ignore any harm that might come to your brain."

"Thank you."

I was well regarded!

I was now able to shift myself to a sitting position on a stair. I had not hit my head. My backside was achy, but I was not in pain. I remembered that I had not become the chaplain of the mason from the roof collapse. I remembered I had slipped on the stairs and fell.

And I walked in the night.

"You said shelter," I told the housekeeper. "What's it called?"

"Oh, Reverend, you've got me there. I'm drawing a blank. It was my daughter who brought me."

"What did it look like?"

"Brick. I recall a brick building. They painted it over with white, but you could still see it was brick. How are you feeling now?"

"I really am all right," I said, concealing my disappointment.

The housekeeper took hold of my hand, enfolding it with both her own, like a sandwich. She helped me up to my feet.

We parted after a quick, warm embrace and an offer from her to have tea together one of these nights, which I accepted. I wasn't so shaky I couldn't continue down the stairs.

"Please still be here," I was saying, like a prayer. "Please please please still be here."

The gray light of dawn was everywhere outside the windows I passed. I could smell breakfast being made below in the kitchen, coffee and bacon and doughy things being baked, overwhelming all the usual smells of the hospital. I felt the day beginning to wake, vibrating all around me. I felt what it's like to know a day is like a country I had to take my leave of.

There they were.

If I hadn't turned a corner that moment, on my way to the consultation room, I would have missed them. They were headed for outdoors: the pregnant handler and the boxer.

"Hey! Eddie!"

He turned his big head. Do animals smile?

Yes they do.

His jowls were relaxed; he was showing a bit of teeth. And there was his tail, going from stillness to the hello of a quick back-and-forth, as a human would wave a hand.

Once, I sat with a man who ran a sanctuary for horses. Some had been in racing, some in the carriage-ride trade, some in circuses. Some were elderly, and turned out of their stables by owners who wanted those stalls and pastures for animals young enough to ride. The man had grown angry in his illness, which had reached a point of being untreatable. He had asked for a chaplain because he wanted to talk about God—but not in relation to how sick he was.

He had left the medical center for hospice care, at the sanctuary. He could prove to me that God does not take part in life on Earth, he had said. All you have to do is think about the fact that animals cannot speak to humans in words. Or to put it another way, humans cannot speak to animals the way animals speak to each other.

Maybe, he had hoped, he'd be lucky after his passing. He wanted to be a ghost with the power of finding out from his horses everything about their lives they had not been able to tell him when he was alive. He wanted to move among them like he was taking notes for their biographies. He wanted to let them know it had sometimes made him yell and kick the ground and raise his fists toward the sky like a bellowing, bearded Old Testament prophet, or a raging old king in something by Shakespeare. "Why," he would yell, "why, why, why can't we walk up to an animal and have a conversation?"

"I wish you could talk, Eddie," I whispered to him, bending to pat him.

He raised his head so I could scruff my fingers at his neck, and pat the white bib of his chest. He sniffed me as if I might have a slice of pizza folded up somewhere in a pocket.

"What's that you said?"

The young woman held his leash with one hand. Her other arm was in a curve at her belly, like a sling. Over her beach ball jersey was a faded-green army-surplus jacket, way too big for her. It was unzipped, though; clearly it couldn't reach around her belly.

"I was just saying hi," I answered. "But I'm wondering, as I'll be seeing him on my shifts, can you tell me anything about where he came from?"

She was impatient to get away. This would be her first baby. She hadn't experienced morning sickness since the first few months, but all the smells of cooking were making her nervous she'd be sick.

She was about to quit her job. She would become a stay-home mom, so when I encountered Eddie again, he'd be with someone else. Right now though, they had a mission. She was wiped out, but they'd been called to another hospital, one that took in other people from the roof collapse. Their ride was coming, was probably there already.

And please, as she'd deliver her baby here, would I come see her?

She was incredibly nervous about the whole birth and parenting thing. She was just talking to her mother the other day and her mother told her horror stories, *horror stories,* of what she went through with her, involving two days of *agony,* and wasn't it terrible for a mother to say to her pregnant child, "You tried to kill me, and I hope yours doesn't do the same"?

In fact for years and years in her childhood, her mother called her "Killer Baby," like that was her actual name. Growing up, she'd been highly active, and for a time, she took lessons in boxing. Also judo. She had never imagined Killer Baby was meant *literally.*

All through the handler's low-volume outburst, Eddie stood solemnly, looking up at me, saying nothing. I was almost getting mad at him for not being a human-talking dog.

"If it's any consolation," I said, "when my mother was pregnant with me, she thought she was entering menopause. I was probably the only first grader in my school who knew that word. But I thought it meant something else."

"Wow, Reverend, is your mom, like, old?"

"She doesn't believe so."

"What did you think menopause meant?"

"A disease you die from, because there isn't a cure," I said.

"Oh, God. But then, it wasn't death. It turned out to be you."

"That's a lovely way to put it. Please, when you come in to have your baby, have me paged."

"What if I come in and it's daytime?"

"They'll call me at home."

"Will they let you in the labor room?"

"I can go anywhere," I said. "Can you tell me about Eddie's background?"

"Sure. But there's not much to know."

"I heard he was a stray."

She nodded, and her expression was very much like the face of the horse man, when he was deeply sad, as an undercoat to his anger.

"Someone found him sleeping under a bush in their neighborhood, Reverend, and lucky for him, they knew about our agency. They had a feeling he'd be good in hospitals."

If Eddie knew he was being talked about, he gave no clue. An intern was walking by with a food tray. A tiny trickle of drool began to appear on his muzzle, and he quickly licked it away.

"Why did they have the feeling?" I said. "Was it a guess? Or was it maybe some instinct?"

"Both, actually. But it was more, he was in rough shape. Someone wasn't good to him. We had a fundraiser for his vet bills. I'd rather not get into the details, okay?"

"I understand."

The handler was patting herself on her belly now. When she said, "Hush, no worries, everything's all right," she was speaking to her baby.

To me she said, "We put up notices all over the place, and online too, about a lost boxer, but we didn't find whomever it was he used to be with. We weren't giving him back, of course. We wanted to have that person arrested. What I'm trying to say is, everyone knew he'd be our new star, because he knows what it's like to be the one in the bed, all hooked up to stuff."

"He doesn't show it."

"No scars, I know. He's a really strong guy."

I was quiet a moment, absorbing this news. Then I said, "I bet you know about all the animal shelter places around here."

"Pretty much."

"Do you know of a place that's sort of isolated? I mean, it's around lots of trees. A wooden structure, cheerful looking. It has walls like a barn. There's a main section and two wings."

"Do you remember it from a long time ago, or something?"

"Kind of," I said. "I don't know its name or where it is exactly."

"Sorry, it's not ringing any bells for me. I really have to leave now. See you later?"

"Yes. I'm sorry I missed Bobo Boy's burial. I wanted to be here."

"It was nice. We brought Eddie and he peed around that tree something like ten times. He's different from Bobo Boy totally. But we try not to compare. Bye, Reverend."

Eddie did not look back at me as he trotted away.

I spotted a woman in Food Services pushing a cart toward an elevator. It was not a food truck for patients. There were bottles of water and plates of fruit and pastries, bound for an early meeting in a conference room. The woman looked friendly, in a middle-age, matronly way. She was crisp and neat in her uniform of loose pants and an overblouse.

Casually, I made it seem I just happened to be headed in that direction.

"Hi, Reverend," the woman said. "You're awful early today."

"I'm on nights now."

"Well, I know who you are. I heard you've been calling May Jeffries at the rehab. She's a real special lady."

"Oh, she is. I wish I could visit her. If only I had more time in my days."

"She knows that," the woman said. "Help yourself! I'm looking the other way!"

The elevator was opening, so I acted fast, snagging water, a banana, and a blueberry muffin. I thanked the woman warmly, then leaned by a window to have this meal standing up.

I made a note to myself to tell May Jeffries about being allowed to steal from the cart. The rehab center where she was a patient was too far away for me to fit in a visit. But I called her every evening, usually as it was getting dark.

This woman's heart had never given her trouble, until it suddenly did. The surgery she required was complicated. When I became her chaplain, post-surgery, she was still in peril, hanging on with everything she had.

What she wanted was a picking up of her spirits. She felt that she and I had something in common. One of us was a feeder of hospital bodies, the other of hospital souls.

"Souls have to eat or else they shrivel like a raisin in the sun," she liked to say.

She belonged to a Baptist church. Her own pastor came often to the medical center—but she wanted me around anyway.

She was in her late fifties. She looked and sounded much, much older. She'd grown up in a world of harshness, of many different kinds of deprivation, and of many harms to her body and soul. Inside herself, she was a cactus in a desert, as she'd put it to me: the kind of cactus that flowers fantastically, but will prick you if you mess with her.

May Jeffries had worked here in Food Services a long time. She supervised tray lines. Under her uniform, she often wore T-shirts bearing the face of Barack Obama—she'd unbutton her top to show it off whenever she had a new one.

When she found out about Guy RN and his name tag, she wanted to wear a big one saying, "Proudly biracial but really BLACK LIKE OBAMA."

But then she had her heart attack.

The chapel was where we met, not long after the renovations. Somehow she'd heard I'd had a hand in that, and she decided to bring me food. Once a week, on Tuesday afternoons, when the kitchen director was absent for a regular upper-staff meeting, I received a phone call from her, instructing me to go to my office. It was a ritual. May Jeffries—and she was always called by her full name—made it seem she had a regular appointment with me, confidentially.

Probably everyone in Pastoral Care knew what was what. In she would come, a very stout woman, wrapped in her beloved, woolly, royal-blue poncho, and bearing the L. L. Bean canvas bag she carried with her everywhere, monogrammed with an "M" and a "J."

In that tote, wrapped in foil, still warm, would be a plate or a bowl of whatever the cooks had made for the kitchen people, in the break between lunch and dinner while their director was away. These meals were most definitely not meals that were given to patients. And there was always a dessert.

"Feed my damn soul and pick up my damn spirits," she had said to me in the ICU. "And don't tell me not to say *damn* to a reverend. They split open my chest. I can say any damn thing I want."

So I talked and talked to her, about all sorts of things— whatever came to me—until I became a listener. I learned that May Jeffries, in all her roundness, all her fleshiness, took sailing lessons in a community boating program at a lake, when all her life previously, her idea of being outdoors was to hurry back inside.

"Fat people can sail," she told me. "The boat didn't sink when I got on."

One day at home, she explained, she was clicking around television shows, as usual. She landed on a program about sailing at the very moment the battery in the remote went dead. She was about to get up off her couch and go find another battery, but instead, she found herself watching the show—really watching it.

Somehow, that program *spoke to her and woke her up.*

She joined the adult swim-lessons program at a YMCA, and stuck up for herself when they wanted to put her in the special water aerobics class for weight-loss people.

Her dream was that, one day, she'd be able to buy herself a Sunfish. You could get them cheaply when the boating program held a sales day for the ones they were cutting from their fleet. She had already decided the colors of the sail: splashes of orange and green and red and yellow, the same colors of the gelatins that went on trays, over and over and over, every day.

I almost had told her that Bobo Boy threw up Jell-O on a patient's bed and tried to eat it. But I stopped myself.

Lately she'd been reading about wind. She'd never been much for cruising around in what she called "Cyberland," but she had a new iPad: a gift from people in the kitchen, which I'd contributed to, because of course they came and hit me up, knowing I was a beneficiary of hers.

Ancient people believed gods were in the wind!

How could she never have known that before?

She loved the prayers and the hymns of her church—the hymns especially—and now she had a whole other addition to the *interior life of her own spirit.* She made a private prayer for herself. She imagined herself a long, long time ago dweller at the side of the same lake where her lessons took place.

Her prayer was addressed to Wind. She had spoken it to me often, sometimes on the phone when she had gone through another bad day in rehab. She felt that ancient people must have been on familiar terms with their gods, seeing as how there were manifestations of them everywhere, and you could see or hear or touch them, or feel them on your skin.

Oh please come on now, Wind, and blow some life into my sails, as I surely can't do it myself, big of a mouth as I have.

I had her voice in my head, saying those words. I found a trash bin and a recycle bin for the banana peel and the water bottle. Then I went online on my phone. I did a search for animal shelters within a wide radius of the medical center. For ten minutes I scrolled and clicked, giving up when it occurred to me I was wasting time. My shift wasn't over. What was I going to do about the broken submarine?

I had no idea. I would have to just hope that the right thing to say would come to me before I returned to the librarian's room. At this moment, in the wake of the prayer of May Jeffries, *life in my sails*, there came to me the memory of another woman who had me paged, to be with her during a time before she delivered her baby.

Two obstetricians I know, married to each other, have a daughter in real estate. This daughter wanted me to sit with her when she was hospitalized for frightening complications. Like the woman with Eddie; it was her first pregnancy.

She didn't want her parents hovering—they knew too much; they could not hide their anxiety. Her husband, an investments banker, had been convicted for some sort of fraud, a shock to them all; her divorce was newly final.

This was, for me, during the time of Green Man, and I was in love. I had just bought a book that was basically an encyclopedia about ancient-to-modern plants that grow in the wild and have medicinal uses. I had brought it to work with me, as if I actually had time to take a break and read. But I had liked to have it in my desk. So I brought it along to the woman's room.

I had thought I might dip into it in case she was napping or drowsed off. But I read aloud to her when she expressed an interest: angelica root, dogbane, woundwort, periwinkle, valerian. I went back the next day, and the day after that, and did the same.

Later, I wasn't sure if I made a difference in what she was going through, but when I visited her as a new mom, her baby in her arms, healthy as healthy can be, she told me that she'd heard from her parents where I lived, and she felt I should quit being someone who rented a little space in a massive complex. I should buy myself a house.

I had not mentioned anything to her about my apartment, or anything about myself at all. The information had come from her parents.

She wanted to find a house for me. She promised she'd never make me go around viewing properties I would never choose to even enter. She'd handle everything, and she'd give me a great deal on her own commission, and I was not to put up an argument about that.

I thanked her. I assured her I did not need a house. I almost blurted it out that I would be living where Green Man was, and why.

I wondered if I still had her card somewhere. But she wouldn't be a problem to find.

It felt strange to think about the future. To have a tiny sort of glimmer I had one.

Twenty-three

I looked in on the surfer and again found a pale thin boy of a sleeper. He didn't know it was morning. His drapes were closed. He didn't know I was watching him.

If his breakfast arrived before he woke, his tray would not be left. He was monitored—as if nurses and aides weren't in and out of his room all the time. When he stirred, he would not be left alone.

I knew from other mornings that when he started waking, drifting in that twilight between the here of the hospital and the there in his head, he didn't immediately remember his brokenness. He didn't know he had traveled east, ascended a rock cliff, stood on a rock that gave way, and stayed alive when no one else did.

It was still all new to him. He wouldn't know what happened to his body until he had to find out all over again. Needing to pee, he would start to make a move to get up, to swing his legs over the edge of the bed, and then his legs would not move.

Sometimes his wailing was high in pitch, as if his voice belonged to a suddenly frightened baby.

Sometimes the wailing was low and choppy, like a boy going through his voice change.

Sometimes, the one at his side when he woke was me.

I thought of Plummy. I almost grabbed my phone to get in touch with him. Not to talk about oobs that weren't oobs, or the submarine movie he loved, or anything else about this night.

And not to talk about "us" and how we needed at last to quit each other.

Germany has mountains! The Alps! I basically don't know anything about geography, but I didn't have to Google "dangerous

cliffs in Germany" to know I was right about that. I felt a powerful desire to tell Plummy to make sure he did not go out somewhere in his faraway country and climb any sort of rocky elevation
whatsoever, even though he'd never even imagine himself doing
such a thing. His idea of doing anything athletic is, having sex.
I wondered if he was sleeping with someone he hadn't told me
about. Maybe a scientist, a logical woman. Maybe one of the neurologists he was consulting with.

I gave myself a poke, back out of my imagination.

On slept the surfer. He was a lonely boy who took to the waves
and found something sacred. Who would love him, after he left
the medical center?

Please someone love this boy, I was saying, as a prayer into the
future.

"Waves are still holy," I whispered to him, like the words could
seep inside him, and stay.

Twenty-four

She was waiting for me in the hall, having somehow tracked me down: a girl of nineteen or so, her presence a shock, like a figure cut out of a painting and placed in another, of a totally different place, a totally different everything. You admired the surprise while being baffled—now I knew why people reacted to Bobo Boy the way they often did. I almost expected the phantom of him to trot toward us, tail up, wagging a greeting. I had the feeling this girl would have seen him as clearly as I would.

Yes, I was the chaplain of the woman from the nursing home who passed away in the night. Did she want to sit somewhere privately with me?

She did not, but thanks for asking. She only had a few minutes to spare. We edged ourselves over to a corner to stay out of the way.

"Are you a reverend, like ordained and everything?"

I nodded.

"You don't look like one."

"You're not the first to say so," I said, warming to her. "Please tell me how I can help you."

"I'm Tiffy," she said.

It was not a statement of introduction. It was a label placed on information she thought I knew.

"Actually, it's Tiffany Dawn. I mean, if that's how she put it. I used to tell her all the time to cut it out. It sounds like a dish detergent. Or one of those horrible room deodorizers you plug into a wall."

"I think it's a pretty name," I said.

"So did she."

I could not tell this girl Mrs. Copp hadn't spoken of her. She seemed so sure. *I'm Tiffy, and of course you know who I am and of course I would take up some space in that old woman's mind in her last hour.*

I said, "Did you come to identify her?"

"Oh, no. That wouldn't be up to me. I caught a ride with them, though."

Was she a member of Mrs. Copp's family?

I did not have the sense her outfit was something thrown together first thing in the morning, maybe after a phone call: hard news, news of a death. I felt she dressed this way regularly. A girlishness was all over her. She was fully still being a teenager, dragging it out about having to grow all the way up. I thought of myself, and what a hurry I'd been in.

And she was beautiful. She was truly, stunningly beautiful. Her voice held no accent. I made a guess that in Mrs. Copp's family a baby had been born whose parents were, one, white, and two, Hispanic, perhaps Puerto Rican.

The fact that I was going to have to lie to her was apparent to me almost immediately. Looking at her was like looking at the child Tony and Maria could have had in *West Side Story,* if they'd run away from home, and if Maria in the movie had been cast as a beautiful woman who was actually Puerto Rican. Which is not to say this girl didn't look a little bit like Natalie Wood. She did.

And she was doing her best to hide it. I was certain she did so on purpose. Nothing about her was insecure, unconfident. I saw a toughness. I saw hurt below the toughness and more toughness below the hurt. I saw self-protectiveness, stubbornness. She wanted me to tell her about Mrs. Copp's death, but not really, not specifics.

She was tall and slender—I had to tip back my head to speak to her. Despite the newness of spring, she wore a short, summery, wide-skirted dress that in a smaller size could have been worn by a little girl decked out for a party. The dress was cheerfully pink, like cotton candy. Her legs were in black tights. Her shoes were Mary Janes. Her jean jacket was baggy and far from clean. Her only makeup was very thick mascara, in what seemed to be multiple layers, expertly applied, and lipstick that looked like too much white coating of a sunblock. Her long, dark hair was held back on the sides with barrettes that displayed her as Goth: wide leather clasp-ons decorated with a silver skull and crossbones.

You might think her ear piercings held earrings that were small silver crosses, but they were daggers. The midline was too high. The points at the bottoms were sharp.

She was asking me, Did Mrs. Copp suffer? Did it happen quickly? Was she freaked out from being brought to a hospital?

"She was peaceful," I said. "It happened a little while after she arrived."

The girl didn't know about the stroke.

"Was it her heart?"

"I'm not sure," I said.

"But you were right there, right?"

"I was. She never left the ER. I knew she didn't want to be admitted as a patient."

"She started to hate hospitals," the girl said. "I don't know why. Did she say?"

I shook my head no, then she smiled for the first time, her white-pasty lips somehow perfectly right.

"The ER's on the first floor," she said. "That means they didn't take her up in an elevator. So she didn't have to hear the ding of her top floor in any hospital. She told you about the elevator, right?"

"We only had a little time."

"Did she tell you I didn't come see her the last two times I said I would?"

I reached out my arm while looking at her directly, watching to see if she was okay with being touched. She was. I placed my hand just below her shoulder, as if I thought she might tip over sideways and needed to be propped.

I took a chance. "She only told me she loved you."

The Goth-girl looked away for a moment. Tiffy. Tiffany Dawn. She didn't cry.

"Really, Reverend, did it happen in, like, peace and quiet?"

"I promise you, yes," I said. "She wasn't in pain or distress. She was a lovely lady and I'm blessed I had the chance to meet her."

"She was funny, too. But maybe that part of her didn't show."

"Oh, but it did. I'll tell you, someone in the ER mistakenly called her Marge, instead of Marjorie."

"She hated that nickname!"

"I know," I said. "So she said to that person, "Hey, do I have blue hair . . .""

I was interrupted. "Like Marge Simpson! Get out! She really said that?"

"She did."

"Oh my God, she loved that show."

I said, "Would you like me to walk with you to meet the folks you came with?"

"Nah, I got it. I'm okay."

She had turned to leave, after giving me another smile.

"Thanks," she said, looking back at me. "I'm glad I found you."

"Me too," I said.

But then I had to catch up with her before she turned a corner and reached a stairwell. It was a good thing she had declined my company. I felt I should avoid stairs, at least for a while.

She knew what I was going to ask. I didn't have the chance to say it.

"When you die, and I don't know how she came up with this, it's like, life has an elevator," the girl said. "It can only go up. When it dings your top floor, it's time to step off. She always said she hoped her ding would be, like, a really sweet sound. Like the sweetest sound there ever could be, and it's only with that one ding."

"I believe it was," I said.

"Yeah, I got that. Thanks again."

And then she was gone. A great-grandchild? A niece of a nephew or niece?

Ding went the elevator I had to ride in. I wondered where Marjorie Copp believed she'd be stepping to. I wished I knew that.

Twenty-five

Once when I was in seminary, a lighting fixture attached to the ceiling went haywire, blinking and sparking and turning brighter for several moments, in some sort of power surge that only affected that one light.

It was an evening class. The windows were bare. The dark, moonless night was pressing hard against the glass, as if it were alive, and trying to come inside. We were exhausted. The class was three hours long. We'd gone into overtime half an hour ago.

The book we were discussing was called something like *A Philosophy of the Soul for Dummies*. It was a collection of arguments that basically laid out the case for its nonexistence, as a thing.

The evidence gathered in the book made sense. The professor weighed in on the side of the authors, like a prosecutor making a case. She was prodding us, and things grew heated. Everyone became an instant philosopher-theologian, quoting all sorts of texts, through *centuries*.

A woman who was also working on a psychology degree said that it's all about having a mind, which of course means a function of your brain, plus your genes, plus where and how you grew up, plus where you went to school, etcetera.

A guy who was auditing the seminar from his program in comparative theology said that he was the son of a hard-core Buddhist and a hard-core Hindu, and he had learned from the experience of growing up that everyone should just plain make up their own minds about what to believe, because you have to believe in *something*, or you'll never want to get out of bed in the morning, and it's all just delusions anyway, which is not to say all delusions are bad.

A former student of physics said it was impossible for her to believe in souls, as she already knew that nothing was real unless you could measure it.

I had thought about telling them about my fairy and my childhood physician and my theory of X-rays, but I didn't. We had reached the point when everyone wanted to call it quits.

But we were not in a state of being fully depressed. Most of us were going to be on very intimate terms with people in the act of leaving life. And people who were suddenly new mourners.

How could we face the mourners of the one who was gone, if all we had, in our own minds, was something like, "Well, an end is an end and that's it, and we're done here"?

Like, "That's it, folks, like the end of a life is the same as the end of an old cartoon, as spoken by Porky Pig"?

Those questions were raised by a woman who was already going out to a hospice care place to shadow actual chaplains. A young Catholic sister from the Philippines, new to our class, and also to America, asked what the woman was talking about, because who is Porky Pig?

So that had to be taken care of. Then someone else, a stocky, balding man in his sixties, about to be ordained after a long career as an investigator with the IRS, talked about how he had scorned all religion when he was a kid, but he changed his mind about believing in souls on the day he turned fifteen.

He didn't call it "believing in souls" right away—that came later.

This man wasn't utterly pessimistic about everything, as a rule. He'd had plenty of proof in his old job that there were more people who do not commit tax fraud than there were people who do. Or so he would continue to believe, he had told us.

On his fifteenth birthday he received as a gift a little blue transistor radio, which he had hoped for, but didn't expect. His family was in dire straits financially. His joy was nearly overwhelming, because at last he could go to school and not be the only kid who didn't know the words to Top Forty songs. But when he turned the

radio on, the first station he came to that wasn't just static was playing a song that freaked him out.

It was the great Peggy Lee, he told us, singing "Is That All
There Is?"

Until that moment, he was a normal kid who thought emptiness
was all about your belly and how it was time for a meal. Or nothing was on television except reruns and the news.

He had felt hollow, just *hollow*, by the time the song finished. It
was hard to describe, except to say he felt that his body was some
kind of barrel, and it was empty, just terribly, completely empty.

"I'm an empty barrel" had seemed to him like something you
shouldn't be saying when you're only fifteen.

Or ever.

In fact that's why he decided to be a minister, after all these
years, like he was finally getting around to it.

To say it was a bummer of a song did not even begin to suggest
what it could do to you. The song haunted him still, and to prove it,
he sang us some lines, in a deep, reverberating, beautiful voice, which
up until then, no one knew he had. It turned out that he belonged to
an a cappella group with friends of his who were still with the IRS.
Singing was a way of coping with life in general, he felt.

He sang,

> *Is that all there is?*
> *Is that all there is?*
> *If that's all there is, my friends,*
> *Then let's keep dancing.*
> *Let's break out the booze*
> *And have a ball.*

Everyone knew it was a coincidence that the light in the ceiling went crazy right afterward. Everyone knew the fixture had
an electrical problem that was equal to an illness, and sooner or
later the maintenance people would take care of it. Of course it

hadn't happened that a soul from who knows where had somehow entered the wires at just that moment to display itself.

But we were all, *Look at that!*

The professor, at the head of our seminar table, stood up. In the hush that came over the room, we forgot about the outside darkness, and the fact that we'd be leaving the building to enter it. We forgot about being exhausted.

"Reverend Professor Pearls," we called her. She was about the same age as the former IRS man. She had a way of being profound and making it look easy, and also of looking elegant all the time, as if the wearing of a black clerical skirt-suit and a full white collar meant the height of dressing well. Once when she was asked why she wore a collar, she said she'd chosen to do so because she grew up in a family where the women were expected to practically never go out of the house without a string of pearls around their necks. She wore her collar as her string of pearls.

Standing there, she glanced up at the ceiling light, tipping her head at the sound of the buzzy sparking, as if to better hear it. She didn't say a word about the "malfunction." She was simply acknowledging it, appreciating it.

She looked at the IRS man. "I feel the same way about that song," she said. "I wonder if anyone can come up with another one, before we call it a night. And let me say, for those of you who'll one day sit with people on their way to leaving this world, please don't have that song in your heads."

There was a silence. No one looked interested in becoming a spontaneous singer.

Then the sister from the Philippines rose to her feet at the other end of the table. She was taking chaplaincy classes in addition to her program in nursing—her order ran clinics and outreach programs in Manila. She was a very small woman of thirty or so, in a blue-and-white habit that was not strictly traditional, but could almost pass as a laywoman's suit. She wore her veil with its white band pushed back on her head; her bangs formed a straight line across her forehead. So far in her brief time with us, she had appeared deeply shy, and easily intimidated, as she was going through a phase of being self-conscious about her English. It was surprising to see her step up like this.

She didn't sing. But she had something to say. She was nervous. The treble of her light, soft voice was a little shaky. She told us she'd never heard of the song, but it scared her.

A solemnness came over us as the sister bowed her head and held up her hands, clasping them together, palm to palm. She was giving us a benediction.

"People are so sad," she said.

"People are so hurt," she said.

"So please let us not be empty like empty barrels," she said.

All along, the ceiling light kept doing its thing. And together with Professor Pearls, we answered her, as if this had been planned, "Amen."

Twenty-six

The overhead light in the librarian's room wasn't going haywire and fizzing, but it was acting up, in random patterns of blinking and going partially dark in little blots, like sunspots.

She was very much awake, sitting up in her daffodil night-gown, freshly bathed and completely ready to tell me what was on her mind. To a casual observer, she seemed like any elderly patient waking around the crack of dawn, waiting for the big event of the arrival of breakfast, still a ways off.

I saw right away that some sort of change had taken place in her since I'd slipped away from her all those hours ago, dragging the weight of having no words to say, feeling I had failed her. But what it was exactly, I didn't know. A brightness was in her eyes I had not seen before.

I did not even receive a hello. Angry as she was, she wasn't let-ting herself slip over an edge into losing her self-control. She was fully the boss of herself, even though she sounded a little lashing and shrill.

Why wasn't anyone from Maintenance coming to fix that light?

Look what was going on! Her own blood was trying to kill her and if that wasn't bad enough, it was taking them forever to dissolve her clot, and she was getting the feeling she'd have been better off if she had called for a *plumber*.

That light was giving her a headache! Eyeballs are not sup-posed to throb and hurt, which hers were doing, for the first time ever! And she was worried about what could happen if she ran out of time, not for the length of her life, but for being here. Any day now the Medicare people would come nosing around, and her insurance people too, because you can't be old and have just

Medicare anymore, because, look at this country! Look how the United States of America is a place where being sick became, Let's give more money to titans of capitalism!

She wasn't any socialist! She was a plain old garden-variety Democrat! She was mad! They count how many days you're a patient, like you checked into a five-star hotel, if five stars are the most a hotel can get, she wouldn't know! Do not even get her going about the medical insurance racket!

And her light was broken! The last straw! Did I ever see those famous videos of the girl parrot who's *mad*? I should check them out sometime. I should Google "angry parrot."

They were a big hit at the assisted living place! In one, the parrot is watching the guy she lives with stomp on a cage and smash it—imagine that, *smashing a cage*. The parrot cusses brilliantly! She flashes her head feathers! She says the F word, again and again and again, and truly, the F word has never been uttered so well!

And today, in case I was missing the point the librarian was trying to make, today had only just started, and already, this was how she felt!

She was the kindred spirit of a girl parrot who used to be inside a cage all the time!

"It's okay," I said to the nurse in the doorway, who looked alarmed, for good reason. "We're just talking."

I sat down in the chair, bedside. I forgot how exhausted I was. It occurred to me that I should have doubts concerning what she'd told me about her years in the back room of her library— that she had never hauled back her arm and hurled a book at someone saying certain things and looking at her a certain way. I saw her shininess. I noticed, for the first time, that a tiny drop of dried blood was inside the tape on her hand that secured the needle for her drip.

The tenderness I felt for this woman was inside me head to feet, like warm melting wax on a candle. This was not how things were supposed to go. I had expected to find her weak and sad and needy and maybe coming out of a dream that was still in the act of frightening her.

Everything I planned to say about the submarine, on my way here, vanished, and didn't matter, as if I had amnesia about it, and that was all right.

She looked at me, not as someone looking at a chaplain for help with her broken soul, but as someone who had once again made her a little breathless, and dry mouthed too. She turned toward the pitcher of water on her bedside table. The cup was empty. I started to rise to fill it for her, but I never made it.

That was when the old man appeared.

I saw that he was a stranger to the librarian. I'd never been his chaplain, but I knew him vaguely. He was a widower who lived alone, and in the last several years he'd been in and out as a patient, like an old car often rattling or wheezing or fully breaking down— but still in pretty good shape overall. Probably there was not one part of his body that had not undergone repairs.

He had a history of being admitted with a spiking fever or some alarming infection, or he'd be close to respiratory failure, and just when it seemed his condition was dire, he'd bounce back up. I had seen him in the past strolling hallways. He'd greet me cheerfully and hold up his hand to his head, telling me with the gesture that he was tipping his hat to me, and it didn't matter that his hat was invisible.

There he was in the doorway. His height was barely five feet. Straight in the spine, and quite solid, he gave the impression he never in his life considered himself unusually short, and if he'd ever been teased or looked down on, well, he'd never walk away from a bully. His very white face had a pinkness, like a brushed-on pastel at his cheekbones, not like from a fever. He was clearly a man who blushes easily and feels proud of it. And that face was as round as a gnome's, as if he'd come to life from standing as a statue in a flower bed. He was grizzled with white-gray stubble that didn't seem pointy and rough, but soft enough to touch. I felt that the sight of him could give just about anyone the urge to go over and pat him.

His striped pajamas were loose and faded, his terrycloth robe well-worn and frayed. His feet were in hospital-issued slippers. But the librarian was looking at him as if she wanted to pat him too—as if this were not a hospital, and he had fixed himself up for a social call.

You'd think she had spent the last several moments speaking to me about something happy.

"Hello!" she said brightly.

And in he came, acknowledging me with a smile and another tip of his hat. He must have been out for a pre-breakfast hallway saunter. The voice of the librarian had beckoned to him.

"Good morning," he said to her, his voice in the roll of a lilt. "I was just after thinking being stuck in this place might be driving me somewhat insane. And you right down the hall all along and I hadn't a clue."

"My goodness!" said the librarian. "Are you Irish?"

"I am."

"Well I never. There were many Irish coming into the library where I worked, for many, many years."

"You're bookish!" said the little old man, glancing at the stack on her table, beside the water pitcher. "As am I!"

"I have always said that except for the writers of my own race," said the librarian, who suddenly had something of a lilt in her voice, "the Irish are the best in the world with the English language."

The old man beamed at her. "And it's a language that wasn't ours to begin with!"

"Likewise!" said the librarian.

The broken light kept on being broken and neither of them cared. I could see that I was being turned into something like a spare tire in a trunk, if this room were a car.

The light overhead kept blinking.

I rose from my chair. I made way for the old man, as he was bound for the table.

"Let me pour you some water," he told the librarian.

Small tremors were in his old hands as he reached for the pitcher, and the librarian was advising him, in murmurs, to be careful, he wouldn't want to spill it.

You'd think that no one had ever before offered her a drink of water. I stayed long enough to watch him hold out the cup to her. He had only filled it about halfway.

Their fingers were brushing each other as I bade them a good-bye, and the librarian glanced at me and held up the hand attached to the drip, in a wave. In all the time I sat with her, I had never seen her raise that arm. All along, before, she had acted like it wasn't really part of her, like it was some sort of dead weight, like something solid that used to be buoyant, but had recently sunk, like it was doomed.

Twenty-seven

It will happen that the painter of the mural in the new wing will not come back to finish the job. Someone in charge of such things will decide that the room of the cloud needed to become storage space. It seemed the new wing was like an addition to a house designed and built before anyone realized there weren't any closets. The walls will be coated with primer, then painted gray.

It will be the same as if it never was.

As if I never stood staring into that room while my plate of food crash-landed and I did not clean up my own mess.

Once when I was still a baby chaplain, I was called to the bedside of a young man diagnosed with an illness that had not been discovered until it was too late. He came to the medical center for a procedure that might have extended the time he had left, but instead, things had grown much worse. When I entered his room, I was joining a vigil for his last hours.

He was a chef who had opened his own restaurant. Until his illness he had been free from medical problems. When I reached his side, he was drifting in and out of wakefulness, with moments of keen alertness.

Previously, in a consultation in the hall, one of the restaurant's waiters told me the moments of alertness were terrible. It was hoped that a chaplain might be able to console him—in fact, when the chef was in college, he had taken many religion classes, and had considered becoming a minister himself. But that was before he started learning how to cook.

"He insists we keep his door open," the waiter told me. "He keeps looking toward the doorway. But we don't know why. Personally, I think something's wrong in his soul."

I hadn't known of the restaurant, but I learned it was a popular bistro, in a neighborhood where the only other restaurants were chains: an Olive Garden, a Ruby Tuesday, a Red Lobster. I also learned that the chef had always been a private sort of person. No one knew about his illness until its signs were showing visibly. He was single, and too busy, he would say, for a relationship. Until he was sick he had spoken of marriage and children like a pot at the end of a rainbow that had not yet formed in the sky.

The chef was surrounded by members of his family and a few other employees. Each time he opened his eyes, he looked toward the doorway with a shiny, glittering hope—an expectation that excited him, then disappointed him, again and again.

It seemed obvious that he was waiting for someone to show up and say good-bye to him. Hanging over the room, combining with the hush and the heaviness, was the feel of someone missing. An old lover? A secret one?

It was impossible not to glance toward that doorway too. All eyes kept turning that way. The distress of his disappointment was awful to see. Had he wronged someone, and felt the need to ask for forgiveness? Had someone wronged him?

All along, the chef's mother sat silently, her hands on him constantly. Her face was the face of someone who had decided to act as if wearing a mask—a mask of smooth, almost elegant composure. He was the baby of his family. Her favorite. Her ex-husband, the chef's father, had remarried long before, but he was present in the group too, standing as a figure in a painting, a small one, in the background.

Perhaps his mother was thinking her own calmness would pass through her hands and enter him.

Do something. That was what everyone seemed to be telling me. I took my place on the opposite side of his bed from his mother.

"Hello, I'm a chaplain here," I said. "I wonder if I'm the sort of minister you'd have been, if you became one. After hearing about you, I think I might be."

He heard me. He was able to speak. It was hard to decipher some of his words, but he was giving it everything he had.

He had no loose ends to tie up, no lover to have one last scene with, no grievance to settle. What he had was a belief. He believed his most regular customers had organized themselves to make a trip to his room all together, as if someone had put together a list of phone numbers, had taken charge of arranging things. Perhaps there were car pools. Perhaps there was a convoy.

He could not understand why the people who loved his food were taking so long to arrive. What he waited for was not the saying of good-byes. It was the pleasure he would feel when those people talked to him. They would describe their most memorable meals. They would tell him how much they would miss his cooking.

I could see that some of the vigil keepers packed into that room were wondering the same thing. How could a group visit be quickly arranged? Who could be called? Was there such a thing anywhere as a list of patrons?

"We love your food," said a young woman, perhaps his sister, her voice trembling, so that the effect she hoped for was lost.

"I remember the first time I ever ate your chicken pot pie," said another young woman, also seeming to be a sister. "It was the first time I ever *liked carrots*. And that crust. You did it *awesomely*."

The chef did not seem to feel that compliments from anyone in the room counted.

I said, leaning in closely to him, "Your customers are on the way. There was a message. They want you to know they're stuck in highway traffic. I'm sure you don't want them to be upset they're not here already. But they're coming."

The peace that descended over the room was like the sound of silence when you've been listening to a relentless, ear-hurting buzz of static. I bowed my head in the moments after his passing, and did not see his mother rising to come around to my side of the bed. She reached me so suddenly, so surprisingly, I had no chance to prepare myself for what was coming.

The mask was gone. The woman's face was an etching of fury: a terrible look of the shock of a brand new grief, too big to be contained. It was the same as if the chaplain in the room was responsible for the breath of her son that was his last.

She towered over me. She spoke in a voice of icy coldness. She was a mother in the insanity of this moment, lashing out.

"Why did you lie to him? What kind of a minister are you? *Why did you tell him a lie?*"

She was raising her arm. I actually thought she might strike me. The waiter I had talked with in the hall implored me to leave, then whispered, "Thank you."

Almost immediately, a nurse was summoning me elsewhere. I never saw anyone connected to the chef again. His restaurant, I soon heard, was shuttered and put up for sale.

And this was the story I planned to tell the librarian. I was so way beyond exhaustion, but I was cocky enough to expect the librarian to praise me for fixing the sickness of her soul. Just like that!

I pictured her face in the act of transforming from a sad and terrible tension to peace, like the face of the chef, because of a lie.

And maybe, if I really got into some energy for storytelling, as her breakfast would be coming and I might stick around, I'd tell her about what happened with a man who came to America to take a job in a company that went bankrupt and folded about an hour after he arrived, and he could find no other work except waitering in a Chinese restaurant. His English was limited. The company had promised him language lessons.

He had to earn the money to get back home. He and I were about the same age.

I still have, in a desk drawer, the card that arrived for me in medical center mail. It's not actually a card but two cut-out panels of a takeout box, written on in blue ink.

The first panel says, "I now return home. Bye to Lady Reverend Minister. Not to forget for all of life. Please to enjoy."

On the second panel is the information that the restaurant, where the sender worked, would give me a free meal. When I cashed it in, they let me keep it. How that man knew the things I liked to order for takeout, I do not know. We hadn't talked about food. I'd never been to the restaurant before.

"This a gift certificate paid for. Please to present at counter. 1 garlic eggplant. 1 fried bean curd, appetizer size. 1 appetizer vegetable dumplings. Little bit spicy only."

The day he left the medical center, I went to his room and found him dressed and ready. Our heights were about the same. Silently, he placed a hand on each of my arms, a little above my elbows, cupping me. He had touched his forehead to mine. Not a word was spoken.

He was attacked late one night just before the restaurant closed. He was the only one in the dining room. A white man who seemed completely nonthreatening began to argue with him about his bill, accusing him of making an error in adding up the total.

The waiter's eyes, this man said, were too slanted to see properly.

The waiter kept his composure when pointing out that the bill had been done by computer. The man became enraged for what he called "talking back to me."

The man had a fold-up knife in his pocket. The stabbing was vicious, leaving multiple wounds. Although the waiter and other employees of the restaurant were able to give thorough descriptions of the assailant, he was never found. Later, the waiter kept telling himself how lucky he was that his attacker did not have a gun.

I sat with him for an hour or so every day for nearly two weeks. He had no medical insurance. His enormous expenses were taken care of through a fund set up by a Chinese American woman who ran a prosperous public relations firm in the same building. She had a table in the restaurant no one else was ever allowed to use.

Early on, in his delirium, the accountant-waiter took my shape in the chair, so shadowy to him, for his wife. I had seen a photo of her, slender and fit, her black hair straight and shiny: my female physical opposite.

The public relations woman didn't come to visit him but she sent her employees, as did the restaurant, so there was often someone around to translate.

His wife hadn't wanted him to try his luck in America, even though he'd been trapped in dull jobs and yearned for his dream of "America" to come true. She had been waiting for him to save enough money for her and their children to join him.

My boss, the Head, came up with the idea to consult a physician from Beijing we both knew, and with her help, I was able (barely) to manage the job of pretending I was sitting with my husband. We had learned from visiting employees that he liked poetry.

I had a couple of index cards on which the Mandarin words were in phonetic English. As advised by the physician, I did not attempt to put into my voice a false accent. The words would work on their own, I was told.

I don't know what poetry the words came from. I was able to say from the shadows around me that inside himself he was as light and airy as a shiny white cloud.

Those three words had stayed with me in a way the others had not—there'd been phrases too about spring, a river, mist at the top of a mountain giving way to the sun.

Funny that I'd forgotten all about them, until this moment.

Shiny white cloud.

"Brains store up words for the time when you need the right ones and you think you don't have any words! Brains are so awesome!"

"Oh, shut up, Plummy, because maybe it wasn't my brain," I was saying, like he was standing beside me.

"Souls are so awesome!" he replied, in just my imagination, once again, running away with me.

I was going to have to do something about him. But what? Text him not to text me anymore? Call him and say we had to let go of each other, a kind of death, like we were clinging to each other in our two different countries, on ex-lover life support?

The last time we saw each other in a video call, it was, of all things, Valentine's Day. I hadn't known all the details about the budget ax, but I knew enough to feel a real sense of doom. I knew that when all the details came out, the changes would be swift, even immediate.

He had timed calling me at home to reach me before I left for my day shift. Somehow what started out sweetly and friend-like collapsed into a fight neither one of us won. He wanted me to say I was sorry for telling him so many times I'd one day be the minister at his wedding to *someone his own age.*

But the age thing wasn't even the thing. Not as far as he was concerned!

What was the matter with me? What was the matter with my brain? How could I be so kind and thoughtful to patients, so just plain nice, then not even care what sort of effect I had on him, in terms of unbelievable things I said? Did I only care about, like, sick people?

Did I honestly think he would stand somewhere in a tux getting married, with me right in front of him, in *vestments,* because, not that he was marrying someone else, screw that, the wedding that never would happen would probably be in a church, probably in Germany, a place he planned to spend the rest of his life in, because I wasn't asking him to please come back?

He was sick of Europe! He wouldn't care if he never traveled anywhere again!

Did I think he'd return to his own country when I was in it, cold-shouldering him, still being a discriminator, just because, when he was a baby, I was double-digits in my age? Did I know what I also was? He would tell me! I was *sexist.* What if he was the woman and I was the guy? I should imagine that!

And he had realized he would have to wait out coming back to America *until I died and he came for my funeral and everyone would wonder who he was.* That is, if he even knew I was dead!

I had to stop him when he lapsed into German, in a sentence with "т-shirt."

He backed up and tried again. Aha! He was thanking me. We were getting to the core of how emotional he was. He loved the shirt. He thought it was a great Valentine present, as if we sent each other Valentine gifts every year.

"You're welcome," I said. "I only told you once I'd marry you someday and I'm sorry. I promise not to ever say it again."

"Officiate!" he shot back. "Not marry! Officiate at some no-way wedding of mine to somebody else."

"Plummy, I have to go to work now."

"How's it going?"

"Not so good."

"Want to talk about it? I'm starting to totally calm down."

"I don't! Bye!"

I didn't tell Plummy I had mailed the т-shirt ages ago. For some reason it had only just reached him.

A lay chaplain who was also a poet, and no longer in our department, had brought it back from a conference, where some other chaplains were poets too. It was gray with white letters, all caps, and under the words, there was a drawing. Then under the drawing was a name, and it was Emily Dickinson, in letters in script.

THE SOUL SHOULD

ALWAYS STAND A

The drawing was of a jar.

The lay chaplain-poet had given it to me as a gift, as a consolation prize, or perhaps from feeling sorry for me. Although it fit me, I'd thought right away of Plummy, for a good reason. He'd put on weight since we were together—which means, he grew all the way up. I would have told him he was looking very attractive, if he hadn't started his fight and called me sexist, never mind that I'm only considerate about patients, which *hurt*.

I was banned from conferences. I had attended one in the middle of America where I'd become distracted from the reason why I was there.

I'd felt that the conference was really about me looking at cornfields, in springtime, the stalks growing higher in front of my eyes, for miles and miles, endlessly, vanishing into the faraway horizon of a flat and beautiful sky.

I had wondered if it makes more sense to say there is infinity, as an actual thing, if you always see a lot of sky. I had thought of Plummy and his roots. I was emailing him descriptions of what I saw, and we were also in touch on our phones.

When I returned to work, I was in trouble. The gathering was prestigious; the Head had to plead with the medical center for the funds so I could go. But I had taken no notes. I could only report on the fields and the sky, and a paper that was presented about statistics, which said that many, many more Americans believe in forevers than Americans who do not.

Surveys had been taken. It really was impressive when the percentages came out, when the Yes people numbered the same as those new ears of corn, and the No people were sort of scant.

One of the respondents to the surveys had said, "Why would anyone not want to believe in their soul going to heaven, when you'll never know you were wrong, being dead?"

I've thought often of those words, and of those in another comment too.

"I never used to believe in having an 'afterlife' until I got a cat and I realized you can't say the word 'tomorrow' to an animal and expect them to know what you mean. Putting two and two together, I was less depressed about having a tomorrow after the end of my life on Earth, which has not been all that great."

No one in my department cared that I said it was the best conference I went to, not even the Head, who usually stuck up for me.

And Plummy had not been impressed by how happy I was in my days in the middle of America, *my soul ajar.* How could I slack off at a conference? I stand around looking at cornfields, and all of a sudden it's okay to slack off?

I would not, I was thinking, tell Plummy the story of the lawyer. I would not tell him about Eddie and me and being out in the air, and how it felt to hear the dog who was almost dying drumming music. Or about any of this strange, strange night.

Yes, I would.

All of it.

No, I wouldn't.

None of it.

The soul should always stand ajar.

Like souls have a door that can shut and might never be opened. Maybe, I felt, I should tell Plummy about the vase of the bug-eyed frog with the red bow tie, in the gift shop window beside the bootie, and see where things went. I didn't know anyone else who would think it was an excellent thing to own. If he had it, I knew, he'd fill it with his crackers shaped like fish. Probably, they didn't have Goldfish in Germany.

Then I wished he had talked to me that day about why he loved the shirt.

The quote could have been any Emily Dickinson line, because once when he was a sophomore in high school, he made a huge mistake, in an English class. They had an American poetry week, based on way-dead writers, as he'd put it, like the Nevermore Raven, and "Blessings on thee, little man/Barefoot boy with cheeks of tan," and "Listen my children and you shall hear/Of the midnight ride of Paul Revere."

He had tuned out but then along came *this other thing*.

Which was part of curriculum and had to be presented. Which the teacher had stated, like an apology. It had seemed to Plummy that the teacher was not a fan of Emily Dickinson.

All the teachers were Mr. or Mrs. or Miss, but not this one. Rick was his name and he was famous for being easy and jokey and cool. Plummy's mistake was that, when Rick called on him, not that he'd put up his hand, he asked a wrong question. Rick must have noticed from his expression that he was having some thoughts, which did not ordinarily take place for Plummy in that class. He was ordered to tell everyone what he was thinking about whatever Emily Dickinson poems they were discussing, and he said, "How come you're all making fun of this stuff like it's weird and makes no sense?"

Everyone thought he was playing the part of the high-IQ geek looking down his nose, faking an understanding, like his question was a lie and he only asked it to be a jerk. He wouldn't tell me how Rick treated him for the rest of that term. Or how his classmates taunted him.

He said it wasn't that big of a deal and he got over it, and he only told me about it at all because he wanted me to know that he knew how to, like, read. Like he wasn't one-dimensional or something.

I had thought the shirt became lost in overseas mail. And I wondered, What look was on his face when he opened that package and saw what it was?

Twenty-eight

It was normal for my parents to be up and about early. I knew they'd had their bikes tuned and were itching to ride, now that the snow was gone. And if not a bike ride, golf. Their club was fully post-winter, and the chill in the new-spring air wouldn't stop them; they had insulated jackets and foot warmers and good gloves.

It wasn't unusual, either, for them to get in touch with me as I was going off a shift. Drive home safely! Call us when you wake up! I knew that they imagined me falling asleep as soon as I landed on my bed. I had decided I would not take sleeping pills. Sometimes, it could be close to noon, or even one, before I finally settled down. It could take me that long to depressurize.

I had just looked at my phone, which I had set on silent.

The first text from them was a simple, "Call us before you leave work."

They were new at this, and didn't quite trust it. The second text was, "Did you see the message we sent?"

The third was, "Call! We have to talk to you!"

The fourth was, "CALL IMMEDIATELY WE LEFT VOICE MAIL TOO IT IS NOT ABOUT ANYTHING THE MATTER WITH US YOU MUST DO SOMETHING SORRY WE KNOW YOU NEED TO GO TO BED BUT DO NOT LEAVE THE HOSPITAL WITHOUT CALLING WHICH YOU HAVE TO DO NOW IT IS VERY IMPORTANT & URGENT."

There were two voice mails, one father, one mother, saying pretty much the same thing.

Yet I was not feeling I had to do as they asked. People in my family are always saying things are urgent when they are not. Once, my parents had me paged when I was on duty in the ER, and it had seemed a crisis was happening with them, much worse than what I was dealing with—and it turned out they wanted to tell me that so much time had gone by since the last time I was over for dinner, they had forgotten what I looked like and had to look at photos of me, and it's not as if they were having memory issues. And I'd been over for dinner not even four days earlier.

They were never to do that again.

I was ready to begin the slog of un-attaching myself from the medical center, then getting myself back to my apartment. It was, Oh, I'll call them later. But then a memory rushed up to me from somewhere deep, as if I had actually summoned it.

There's a photograph.

In the photo, I'm six, a first grader. The photo is in a frame, hanging on the wall of the house I grew up in, in the upstairs hallway, along with others of my sister and brothers at around the same age.

The three of them are seen in action, outdoors: on child-size skis, kicking a soccer ball, riding a bike. The one of me has me inside, wearing shorts and a T-shirt, in the same hallway.

I had not known it was being taken. It was a surprise when I saw it later, but I never wanted to get rid of it. I loved having it framed there, odd as it made me seem. In fact when I was home saying good-bye before leaving for seminary, I climbed the stairs to say bye to the photo too. I had spoken to the girl who was me.

"I promise to be the sort of minister you would approve of," I had told her. "I promise I will never do my work like I'm some kind of robot."

It was almost summer when the photo happened. There was an end-of-the-year school show with a theme of, "Let's all think happy thoughts today and be happy."

Maybe it wasn't exactly in those words, but that was the gist of it. Early on in the show, the first grade went onstage to lead an audience sing-along of "If You're Happy and You Know It, Clap Your Hands (Clap, Clap)."

I was supposed to be in the back row, but things became chaotic when we were taking our places. Somehow I was pushed to the front—to the center, where I ended up standing several inches ahead of everyone else, so it appeared I was meant to have a solo, to perhaps be the star of the performance.

I did not want that spot. That spot was all wrong. But when I tried to step back, I found that the front line was too packed with kids, shoulder to shoulder. Because something was happening we had not rehearsed, those kids all decided to just stick with the routine. No one was willing to make room for me, to let me slip to the rear where I belonged. I was trapped.

I did not have worries about knowing the song. I'd known it for forever, and I had kept it to myself that I thought it was too immature for six-year-olds. I had felt it was a song for babies who don't know how to walk yet.

My problem was with the moves. In addition to the physical motions the song called for—clapping, stomping one's feet, all of it—we were required to move our shoulders up and down, and bob our heads like saying yes, and lean a little bit forward then a little bit back, at a tilt, which our teacher called "choreography." Everyone had to make these extra moves in exactly the right pattern, exactly the same way, at exactly the same moments.

There was nothing I could do about the fact that I had come to decide at the age of six that this particular business of "choreography" was bad not only for me, but for all of my class.

I knew what a robot was. Why were we forced to act like robots?

What about the theme of the show? How could anyone be happy in a happy song when everyone was afraid of doing something wrong, all because of the extra moves? It wasn't fun to have to perform those moves. No one smiled in the rehearsals. Everyone knew that if you didn't keep track of when to do what, hard as you were trying to concentrate, the music would stop and everyone would look at you like you'd done something terrible, like peed in your pants.

The song had a built-in choreography to begin with, I felt, with an excellent set of moves, as natural as anything. When you clapped and stomped and all the rest of it, your joy was coming from the inside out. But the teacher was new. She didn't seem to notice she was banishing something natural and joyous. She never instructed us to make sure we kept our souls out of our performance, not in actual words. But we all got that message anyway.

I had memorized all the extra moves pretty quickly. I just couldn't make myself carry them out, which was why I'd been placed in the rear. The teacher had explained that the back row was for the kids *who failed to meet the right standard*.

And there I stood, frozen, trapped, in a spotlight, if a spotlight had been shining. I looked out at the rows of chairs filled with parents, and of course, there were mine, way back in the back, because my father is so big and so broad, he had worried that people sitting behind them might complain about being blocked. It was the first time I was on a stage. I hadn't told them what the song was, or what was required.

At the piano, the teacher playing the song was starting it up, and I realized that if I didn't take action to unfreeze myself and get out of there, I was going to die.

I was not in a panic. I was calm. I saw that my parents were beginning to look like they suspected something was wrong.

I don't know how much of the song took place while I was rigid as steel, my arms at my sides, the air in my mouth feeling like it was maybe my last-ever breath, sucked in but never let out. I felt that my death on the stage wouldn't hurt. It would only be a holding of breath, and then a next one would never arrive, as simply as anything there ever was.

Probably, there were teachers doing their best to signal to me to perform. Probably, my own teacher was appalled, was trying to figure out what to do without screaming at me, as she was sometimes in our classroom a screamer, but not so loud it went anywhere for others to hear.

Then I saw the hands of my mother and father in an act of spontaneous choreography. At first it looked like they were waving to me. They weren't. They were summoning me. I could have been a player on a field, being called by coaches to the bench.

I stepped forward to the edge of the stage, and jumped off. My great good luck was that I landed upright. I wasn't even wobbling.

The song, the routine, went on undisturbed. The singing and the music were at my back as I walked down the auditorium aisle. I was glad I wasn't dead.

But I was mad too. I had lost my chance to sing that song with the other back-row kids, even though it was so babyish. I had wanted to clap. I had wanted to stomp. I had wanted to make the natural moves and be happy and feel my soul, wide awake, zooming around inside me.

The photo happened a little while after we all arrived home.

My father snapped it, having rushed upstairs when they heard what I was up to. I have one foot slightly raised, in a pre-stomping. My arms are spread out wide, the better to clap the next clapping as loudly as possible. My head is tipped back a little, my mouth wide open, my hair wild with frizz. My eyes are closed, because I used to think that's what you needed to do when you're having a moment alone with your own soul.

"Well, you'll never have to worry about anyone turning you into a robot," my mother said, when the photo was framed and hung. I had told them the whole story.

"That was a great jump off the stage," said my father. "That was an Olympic-level jump."

And so I called them, standing by a hallway window, looking out at the morning, watching day-shift people arriving.

"Hi, Mom. Hi, Dad," I was saying. They still had a landline: a wall phone in the kitchen, portable extensions in three other rooms.

And I was saying, "What do you need me to do?"

Twenty-nine

A professional golfer had entered hospice care at her vacation home, on the side of a lake I'd never heard of. The golfer was asking for a minister, when all her life she had sworn she had no interest in anything to do with church.

The golfer didn't say which type of minister she wanted. She only asked that it wouldn't be someone who believed you should do to your soul what another pro golfer had suggested she do with her body.

Her experience with that other golfer was the thing that made her famous, in a way her career and many tournament wins never did. In a contest to raise charity money, she had competed on a fairway, then a putting green, one on one, in front of television cameras and a large crowd of spectators, with an extremely good-looking man who was much younger than she was. A sports journalist who often mentioned Shakespeare characters in his columns started calling him the Romeo of the golf world, and it stuck.

He was enormously popular. In the lead-up to the event, Romeo told reporters he welcomed the chance to show how gallant he was—that was the word he decided on. "I plan to be gallant," he kept saying.

There were interviews with him, although not with her, except for one or two in local papers, in which she was asked if she felt nervous, or if she felt she was staging an event for the sake of publicity for herself. Or if she intended to back out, having concluded she would only be embarrassed, and perhaps do damage to all women in all sports.

Romeo stressed in his interviews that, in such a mismatch of strength and abilities, he intended to focus on his own swinging and hitting, as an exhibition of the beauty of golf. He wasn't looking to lord it over someone he'd of course defeat—not that "defeat" was the right word, since it wouldn't be much of a contest.

When it was over, and his loss wasn't close, he uttered his famous remark. He realized too late it was picked up on a live feed. He seemed to feel that he'd been unable to perform at his best for this reason: he had been bothered very much by the physical shape of the woman who had just shown the world that she could out-swing him, out-hit him.

It was a fact that, at the time of the contest, the golfer did not have the usual body of an athlete. She was no longer young, and she was fleshy, especially around her middle, and she sweated heavily and acted proud of it; her caddy kept towels handy. Walking the greens, she often ran out of breath.

Yet no one had ever gone public in making fun of her. Romeo tried to explain later that he'd been worried she might have a heart attack, or she might faint and collapse. But the truth was plain to see. He really didn't like it that he was looking the whole time at a woman who did not look and act as he felt a woman should, and she was *creaming* him.

"For God's sake, you need to start wearing a girdle," Romeo said to the golfer, even though he seemed too young to know what a girdle even was.

In answer, the golfer looked at the putter she was holding, at the iron of it, and then she raised it, not angrily, not in a fit of temper, but quite serenely.

It really did seem she was going to crash it against his head. It really seemed he understood he was now in mortal peril, and he was taking a moment to try deciding if he had time to flee her, or maybe raise his arms defensively. He looked very, very afraid, and also very surprised.

When she lowered that weapon, and casually handed it to her caddy, and strolled away, she had made herself, as it was often said, immortal.

And suddenly she was dying, and she was afraid.

How could a minister be found who would not make her feel that someone was telling her to wear a girdle on her soul? The hospice organization running her care couldn't promise to help. The request was too unusual. Her personal assistant, tapping frantically on her keyboard, found two nearby hospitals employing nondenominational chaplains. But they couldn't be spared for a home visit, especially in such an out-of-the-way place.

Calls were made to parishes that seemed to fit the golfer's desire. Maybe the assistant didn't do a good job describing the type of person being sought. Maybe everyone contacted just didn't have the time to make the journey to her home.

The only local people connected to the golfer were staffers of hers: a housekeeper, cleaning people, yard-work people. They had all been with her for all the years she owned that property; they knew her well. They were going about their work in the numbness of the dark, awful reality that had settled into the house. The golfer had been so strong, so alive, no one could come to terms with what was happening. Her illness had seemed like something to be swung at, as if the hit on the side of the head she had not delivered to Romeo was meant instead for the thing called Death, gathering itself all around her.

Her staffers did not come up with suggestions. There were no neighbors to consult—the golfer's home was in a maze of private roads. People who owned houses nearby tended only to come in the summer.

She had not made friends in the area. She had not been in the habit of going out to many places.

She wasn't someone my parents knew personally. But for many years, before her illness made playing impossible, she had sometimes turned up at their club, as the only famous person who ever did. Although she kept to herself, and refused to pose for photos, and never attended anything she was invited to, everyone there was crazy about her. And she was generous with caddies, which counted for a lot.

Her longtime business manager was staying at her home along with the people who were closest to her. He had arrived at the point when the golfer's request turned into a demand, and the only thing she would speak of. Everyone in the house was talking about finding a random person willing to accept payment to impersonate a member of the clergy.

That idea was appalling to the manager. He knew that, even under heavy medication, the golfer could not be fooled.

In the night, probably around the time I was entering the mason's room and being rejected, the golfer woke and claimed she felt better than she had felt in months—and she believed that she had summoned perhaps a last surge of energy inside herself, and she wanted a minister more than ever. She wanted to talk about her whole life, she explained, with someone who would come to her side just purely for the sake of her soul.

At some point, her manager had the idea of getting in touch with someone high up in my parents' club, and never mind it wasn't even yet dawn.

He had gone to the club with the golfer when he vacationed at the lake. After her illness fully took her over, and she withdrew from the outside world, he went there on his own. He didn't play, but he always enjoyed a long lunch, followed by an afternoon in the bar, where a section was set aside for relaxing in comfortable armchairs. It seemed reasonable to him to hope that a member of the club would turn out to be a member of the clergy.

The director of the club was the first one he tried to reach, at home. The man's wife was gracious about being disturbed. But her husband, she explained, had been suffering from one of his bouts of insomnia, and only a little while ago he'd taken sleeping pills. She knew from past experience she'd have more success waking someone dead than waking him, and if she did, he'd be so groggy, the manager would have to give up trying to get through to him. She herself didn't know of any ministers. She only went to the club for functions she had to help host, and she rarely interacted with members. She had heard quite enough about golf and golfers as it was.

But the wife called back. She advised the manager to try the membership director, who as it happened was someone the wife did not get along with, or she'd be making the call herself.

The manager did so. His call went to voice mail. But it was returned a few minutes later.

The membership director agreed to handle *this distressing situation*. To her, the golfer was a superstar. She only wished she could send someone who could make it happen that the golfer had many more years to be alive, and to keep showing up at the club.

This was a woman who swore every year that she was about to retire, and then once again she didn't. She knew everything about everyone.

Soon she was waking up my parents.

"Tell your daughter they'll send a car for her where she is. And tell her thank you from the club, even though she hasn't been here since she was little, and she didn't like our Christmas parties because the presents were golf things, which by the way I never forgot."

I went back to my office. Once again, no one was there. I always had a clean change of clothes in a drawer of my file cabinet, folded up as if meant for a suitcase, and fresh collars too. I changed fast. I had a toothbrush and toothpaste in my desk. In our bathroom, I splashed water on my face, brushed my teeth, and did not have a hairbrush right there, so I never minded about my hair. Not that it shows if it's brushed or not.

From a drawer of my desk that doesn't hold anything else, I retrieved my favorite stole, a brightly colored one, a gift from my sister and brothers when I was still in seminary. They had actually gone into a shop together, which they'd had to drive a long way to do. It's a white satin strip of a banner embroidered in different shades of green, bright yellow, bright blue, bright red.

I folded it gently, then tucked it in the compartment of my handbag that's only for my stoles.

They had told me the driver would pull up by the main entrance, which was newly unlocked from the night.

And there was the car. I had guessed they'd send a town car, like an upgrade of a basic taxi. It turned out to be a Land Rover suv, the very most expensive one, gleaming and proud of itself in its body of black and silver.

I was stricken with awe. I'd never had the chance to ride in something so large and so luxurious. I climbed into the back to what felt like an ultra-plush couch of leather, as creamy and smooth to the touch as it was creamy in color.

After the night I'd been through, I did not feel guilty for suddenly loving the word "luxury," instead of thinking about things such as fuel efficiency and the tremendous amount of money spent on this mode of transportation, when a compact hybrid like my own car would get me to my destination just fine.

I leaned back. I was falling asleep before I knew it, falling into a dark and beautiful tranquility, like arms were circling me, and the arms were soft as pillows.

Thirty

A little over an hour and a half later, I woke up. The car had come to a stop. Before my eyes were all the way open, I knew we had not reached the home of the golfer. No houses were visible, no lake.

I blinked myself into an alertness, the same as if I'd dozed off in a bedside chair. The car was at the side of a narrow, unpaved country road bordered by trees, mostly high old maples.

It was only just barely a road; it could have been someone's long driveway. The Rover's engine was still going, in a softly contented hum that was almost a purr.

My driver was an almost-elderly man, lean and sharp-featured, wearing a tweed cap and navy blazer. He was clear when I climbed aboard he did not welcome conversations with passengers, not that he said in words that we needed to ignore each other.

I learned, though, as we were pulling away from the medical center, that he didn't know the golfer, or anything about her. He didn't even know she was a golfer. All he had was an address. I had made the mistake of thinking he was one of her staffers.

He had informed me that the company he drove for had a fleet that was mostly limousines. He'd been on call for short-notice transports. When they assigned him the Rover and sent him to the medical center, he figured he'd be picking up a high-powered executive or very rich doctor.

That explained why he looked surprised when I appeared in a collar.

And now he had turned in his seat to speak to me. My impression of him as a gruff, stern man proved wrong.

"You turned off the ringer," he said. "On your phone. They had to call me instead. You were too asleep to hear it. There was a message from them at the house. I have to tell you, she changed her mind."

"I'm sorry. I'm not following you. What are you talking about?"

"She changed her mind. I'm under orders to bring you back to where I picked you up. I pulled off to turn around. Then I thought I'd better stop a minute. I was thinking about, you'd want to know we have a different plan now. I would've woke you, if you didn't wake up on your own."

"Thanks," I said.

"You're welcome. Heck of a thing it'd be, if you woke up and we were back where we started."

"She changed her mind?"

"That's what they said. I guess it's a pretty big deal. Unexpected, like."

If he told me the golfer had died as I was traveling toward her, I would have bowed my head to honor the passing. But this felt wrong in a very wrong way.

"Are we far from her house?"

"Ten minutes, give or take. Why do you want to know, if it's canceled?"

"I was feeling curious. I'm not sure where we are."

"Are you a pastor?"

"I'm a minister."

"Well, that would mean Protestant. Like it would have to."

"Yes."

"I've heard that Protestants hate it when Catholics call everyone that's a Protestant, a Protestant. Instead of, like, the individual denominations. Like Protestant is all one thing."

I was grateful to him. I knew he was waiting for me to confirm the new plan. He was, after all, temporarily my chauffeur. But I couldn't bring myself to.

All along, the engine was pulsing, in what felt to me now like a tender background humming. When the driver swished down his window, the scents of clean spring watery air blew in on a faint little breeze.

"So, you're Catholic," I said.

"Was," he answered. "Maybe I still am. I don't know. They closed down my parish. It was a bankruptcy. I don't like to discuss it, but I'll tell you, I drove a rabbi to a wedding a couple weeks ago. She was a woman too. When she was finished and it was time to go, she handed me what I think was the most incredible plate of food I ever ate, all wrapped up. If I told you it was gourmet, that wouldn't be the half of it. It was *deluxe*. There was cake too, six layers, every one of them different. I don't as a rule like pastries. Never in my life had a sweet tooth. But I will never forget that cake."

I sat there on the cream-colored seat that didn't feel as profoundly comfortable as it did before.

I said quietly, "Where you were taking me, where the woman changed her mind, it's not for a wedding."

He understood what I was telling him. He was still at an angle to me, leaning in toward the back. I saw him cross himself, touching his fingers to his forehead, his chest, his left shoulder, then his right. I saw that the gesture came swiftly, and almost, to him, unconsciously, as if done by pure instinct.

He asked me, "Do you spend a lot of time with people that are making the crossing over?"

"Yes."

"I used to drive a hearse, for years and years," he said. "Most of my passengers, they don't want to hear about it. But I've got loads of stories. Me and the rabbi I was telling you about, we really got into it. She had stories too."

"Well, we have a drive ahead of us, and I'm awake."

"You work at the medical center?"

"I'm a chaplain there."

"When I picked you up, were you coming off a night shift?"

"Does it show?"

"Kind of, but only before your nap. I'm just saying, I won't take it personal on the way back if you nod off."

That was when the pair of cats appeared in the road ahead, coming toward the car: two calicos, tails in the air, out in the sun to check out their world, one plump, one lean.

I looked at the trees on either side of the Rover. I looked again at the cats. I looked at the narrowness of the dirt road. There came over me a powerful burst of heat, like something inside me had just heated up, like a sunburn or rash, but on the other side of my skin.

I had to get out of that car. Somehow I kept my voice normal, steady, calm.

"Would you mind if I take a walk, before we go back? I'll just go a little way."

"No problem. Go for it. I'll catch a few winks. Stretch your legs. I'm paid by the hour, and they didn't say I had to hurry about bringing you back where I got you."

When I left the car, the cats stared at me in silence, then arched up their backs. As soon as they saw I was walking their way, they turned and fled beyond the trees.

"You're a lane," I was saying to the road. "You're a *lane*."

I did not hear dogs barking. But I hadn't been heard yet: the approach of a human, the opening of the door to the reception area. It was probably their breakfast time. Multiple staffers would be present, like an any normal morning.

The woman asleep in the parlor might have gone home. The dog who lay on the floor might not still be there. Someone might be cleaning that parlor.

There was a bend in the lane, a half-circle. My feet were crunching along on pebbles. The ground, I saw, had once been covered with gravel. Much of it had scattered, either worn or washed away. I didn't notice that when I was here before, but then, I wouldn't have. I had not been touching the ground.

When I cleared the bend, I could only make out an edge of the building's front section. It looked to be the corner where the wing of the cats and the parlor stretched back. I saw the plain simplicity of wooden boards. I knew I was about to see those curtains again, covered with dogs that look like Teletubbies.

I made myself slow down. I was getting excited. I could not enter that building in an emotional way. I thought of the lawyer. I thought of his calmness when he told me his story. I thought of how logical he was. I thought of how I didn't go back to his room to speak to him again before he left the hospital. I thought of how it might have really happened that he rose up in his spirit and walked through his maze and reached the same room I had reached, with its beautiful cloud. I thought of how he would never be saying, "That's it? Just paint on a wall?"

The sound of the Rover's horn hit me with the force of a punch.

"It's on again! They just called me!"

The driver's voice was a bellow, a clarion, a piece of thunder.

"Reverend! Are you hearing me? The lady changed her mind again! She just got nervous! Or shy or something! She's sitting up and she wants you! She's sorry she caused a fuss!"

I froze where I stood, one foot raised in the act of stepping forward. I had the feeling I had to work hard to get it back down.

"Reverend! Come on! She's waiting for you!"

The barking from up ahead came a little muffled. The sounds of one dog gave way a moment later to more: two, three, and then I couldn't tell how many. Their voices were big, deep, small, yappy, all combined: a chorus, filling the air.

I was ready to rush forward, kicking up my feet like an athlete, a racer. Yet I paused. It was just like what happened with the teller's wrong angel. Where should I put myself? Really, how is anyone ever supposed to know where to go?

Forward or back, forward or back?

Then everything felt solemn to me. The joy of my excitement crested in me like an ocean wave, then gently rolled to a rest, like a wave on a shore that sticks around for a while before pulling away. I turned myself around.

The driver opened the door so I could ride up front with him. I accepted the invitation, but first I went into the back to get my phone.

"I sure hope no dogs come chasing us," he said.

"There's a building. I think they're inside," I said, buckling the seat belt.

"I can drive fast, even on roads like these. I'm still making up from the days I went slow with the hearse. In other words, Reverend, hang on."

He backed the Rover out of the lane, then swerved so abruptly, it seemed we were tilting, rolling forward on two wheels only. We turned corners in that maze of back roads. The air grew more watery, and I could see the wide open sky above the lake, blue mixed with gray, air on water, curls of clouds here and there doing slow-motion floating.

It was afternoon in Germany. I only had a minute. My fingers were a little shaky. It wasn't only from the ride. What to say? What to say? What to say?

I decided to be casual about it. Like it was no big deal.

"Hey, there's a frog in a red bow tie I have to buy for you," I typed. "But it could break, so I'm scared about mailing. Talk later? I'm still on duty—overtime."

I shut off my phone again. I thought about how it felt to be small and wild, running around in wet grass of a green, as barefoot as if I'd never in my life worn socks or shoes. Clouds of morning fog came into my hair, and all over me, and some geese would run by, or flap and rise and fly, being chased by the grounds crew, and I'd fall to the ground. Or I'd fling myself down like I was unbreakable, and I'd roll around and get up and run again, like that was my sport, and I was never so alive in all of myself as I was when I was playing it.

I remembered the smell of the grass, the dew, the goose poop, the damp sand of a trap. I remembered a sky wide open, no buildings anywhere, the clubhouse far away, the fog turning shiny as sunlight broke through.

Then I went about recalling everything I knew about golf. I needed to run through in my head the words I'd picked up all my life from my family: irons, woods, tee, putter, birdie, par, bogey, mulligan, slice. I needed to take a deep breath, getting ready to do my job.

Discussion Guide

Do you have a favorite character or patient? Which one, and why? What made them feel real to you?

How do you respond to the chaplain's relationships with Plummy and Green Man? What role do you think they play in the chaplain's work, and in the story?

The chaplain talks often of "doing her job," and she also frequently references her patients' occupations. Why do you think this is? What do you think the novel says about people, their work, and how they do it?

Although the chaplain is not a medical doctor, the work she does is understood as a crucial form of care. Patients and their loved ones depend on her companionship and wisdom nearly as much as the scientific and technical work of the medical staff that saves physical lives. Why is this type of care so essential, and where do you see the chaplain proving that her work is necessary? What does spiritual or emotional care look like for you?

Reason and spirituality coexist in this novel, though they are often treated as opposites. Instead of being disappointed when the explanation for an unusual circumstance is simple coincidence, the chaplain understands that even in those coincidences, revelatory possibility exists. What moments of striking coincidence were meaningful to you in this book? How does the chaplain's perspective on spirituality and coincidence resonate with yours?

The chaplain holds deep reverence for the differences in beliefs between each person whose bedside she visits. These patients' versions of what heaven or the afterlife look like are each unique to their own experiences. Which of these versions were memorable to you, and what details made them so? What does an afterlife look like if you imagine it for yourself?

In a moment of desperation as she sits with an elderly man in distress, the chaplain asks herself, "How can a soul speak to another soul?" Connecting with others without relying on words is a talent of the chaplain's, and part of what makes her work so essential. Where did you notice these moments of connection without language? Have you ever experienced a sense of shared feeling with a stranger?

Coffee House Press began as a small letterpress operation in 1972 and has grown into an internationally renowned nonprofit publisher of literary fiction, essay, poetry, and other work that doesn't fit neatly into genre categories.

Coffee House is both a publisher and an arts organization. Through our *Books in Action* program and publications, we've become interdisciplinary collaborators and incubators for new work and audience experiences. Our vision for the future is one where a publisher is a catalyst and connector.

LITERATURE
is not the same thing as
PUBLISHING

Funder Acknowledgments

Coffee House Press is an internationally renowned independent book publisher and arts nonprofit based in Minneapolis, MN; through its literary publications and *Books in Action* program, Coffee House acts as a catalyst and connector—between authors and readers, ideas and resources, creativity and community, inspiration and action.

Coffee House Press books are made possible through the generous support of grants and donations from corporations, state and federal grant programs, family foundations, and the many individuals who believe in the transformational power of literature. This activity is made possible by the voters of Minnesota through a Minnesota State Arts Board Operating Support grant, thanks to the legislative appropriation from the Arts and Cultural Heritage Fund. Coffee House also receives major operating support from the Amazon Literary Partnership, Jerome Foundation, McKnight Foundation, Target Foundation, and the National Endowment for the Arts (NEA). To find out more about how NEA grants impact individuals and communities, visit www.arts.gov.

Coffee House Press receives additional support from the Elmer L. & Eleanor J. Andersen Foundation; the David & Mary Anderson Family Foundation; Bookmobile; Dorsey & Whitney LLP; Foundation Technologies; Fredrikson & Byron, P.A.; the Fringe Foundation; Kenneth Koch Literary Estate; the Matching Grant Program Fund of the Minneapolis Foundation; Mr. Pancks' Fund in memory of Graham Kimpton; the Schwab Charitable Fund; Schwegman, Lundberg & Woessner, P.A.; the Silicon Valley Community Foundation; and the U.S. Bank Foundation.

The Publisher's Circle of Coffee House Press

Publisher's Circle members make significant contributions to Coffee House Press's annual giving campaign. Understanding that a strong financial base is necessary for the press to meet the challenges and opportunities that arise each year, this group plays a crucial part in the success of Coffee House's mission.

Recent Publisher's Circle members include many anonymous donors, Patricia A. Beithon, the E. Thomas Binger & Rebecca Rand Fund of the Minneapolis Foundation, Andrew Brantingham, Dave & Kelli Cloutier, Louise Copeland, Jane Dalrymple-Hollo & Stephen Parlato, Mary Ebert & Paul Stembler, Kaywin Feldman & Jim Lutz, Chris Fischbach & Katie Dublinski, Sally French, Jocelyn Hale & Glenn Miller, the Rehael Fund-Roger Hale/Nor Hall of the Minneapolis Foundation, Randy Hartten & Ron Lotz, Dylan Hicks & Nina Hale, William Hardacker, Randall Heath, Jeffrey Hom, Carl & Heidi Horsch, the Amy L. Hubbard & Geoffrey J. Kehoe Fund, Kenneth & Susan Kahn, Stephen & Isabel Keating, Julia Klein, the Kenneth Koch Literary Estate, Cinda Kornblum, Jennifer Kwon Dobbs & Stefan Liess, the Lambert Family Foundation, the Lenfestey Family Foundation, Joy Linsday Crow, Sarah Lutman & Rob Rudolph, the Carol & Aaron Mack Charitable Fund of the Minneapolis Foundation, George & Olga Mack, Joshua Mack & Ron Warren, Gillian McCain, Malcolm S. McDermid & Katie Windle, Mary & Malcolm McDermid, Sjur Midness & Briar Andresen, Daniel N. Smith III & Maureen Millea Smith, Peter Nelson & Jennifer Swenson, Enrique & Jennifer Olivarez, Alan Polsky, Robin Preble, Alexis Scott, Ruth Stricker Dayton, Jeffrey Sugerman & Sarah Schultz, Nan G. Swid, Kenneth Thorp in memory of Allan Kornblum & Rochelle Ratner, Patricia Tilton, Stu Wilson & Melissa Barker, Warren D. Woessner & Iris C. Freeman, and Margaret Wurtele.

For more information about the Publisher's Circle
and other ways to support Coffee House Press books, authors,
and activities, please visit www.coffeehousepress.org/pages/donate
or contact us at info@coffeehousepress.org.

Ellen Cooney is the author of nine previous novels, including *The Mountaintop School for Dogs and Other Second Chances* (Mariner Books, 2014). Her stories have appeared in the *New Yorker, Ontario Review, New England Review,* and many other journals. She has received fellowships from the National Endowment for the Arts and the Massachusetts Artists Foundation, and has taught creative writing at Boston College, at the Harvard Extension School, and, most recently, at MIT as a writer in residence. A native of Massachusetts, she lives on the Phippsburg Peninsula in midcoast Maine. Find out more at ellencooney.com.

One Night Two Souls Went Walking was designed by
Bookmobile Design & Digital Publisher Services.
Text is set in Adobe Caslon Pro.